HUMPTY DUMPTY GOES KERSPLAT

HUMPTY DUMPTY GOES KERSPLAT

Gary Alexander

The New Atlantian Library

THE NEW ATLANTIAN LIBRARY
is an imprint of
ABSOLUTELY AMAZING eBOOKS

Published by Whiz Bang LLC, 926 Truman Avenue, Key West, Florida 33040, USA.

Humpty Dumpty Goes Kersplat copyright © 2017 by Gary Alexander. Electronic compilation/ paperback edition copyright © 2017 by Whiz Bang LLC.

For information contact:
Publisher@AbsolutelyAmazingEbooks.com
ISBN-13: 978-1945772528 (The New Atlantian LIbrary)
ISBN-10: 1945772522

HUMPTY DUMPTY GOES KERSPLAT

Humpty-Dumpty sat on a wall,
Humpty-Dumpty had a great fall;
Threescore men and threescore more,
Cannot place Humpty-Dumpty as he
was before.

- Mother Goose's Nursery Rhymes
 Alfred A. Knopf, 1993

Chapter 1

Brick Bates

I WAS YOUNGER THEN, in the summer of 1957. A whole lot younger.

Elvis and Lucy were bigger than big, and cars were just plain huge. Computers were the size of those cars, used as much juice as a neighborhood, and did little. *The Adventures of Ozzie and Harriet* was as close as it got to reality TV. Smoking was cool, not lethal, and seat belts would not have been worn even if cars came equipped with them.

I, Brick Bates, was the greenest private investigator at the Aalborg Detective Agency that I would later come to own. This was why I'd been assigned the Herbie Barnwell case, a nuisance file that promised practically nil in either billing or a satisfactory solution.

In my initial job interview a few weeks earlier, Buck and Spike, the agency owners, spoke reverently of the agency founder, Mr. Linus Aalborg, a remarkable man of Scandinavian descent. A world-caliber decathlete and archer, he had gone off to serve his country in an unknown capacity and never returned, his fate unknown.

A man who could have chosen to ride a desk throughout the war, Linus Aalborg had chosen the precarious existence of a commando. Framed quotes extracted from his infrequent and terse letters home and to his detective colleagues filled the walls of the agency's lobby. Letters that had been turned over to the War Department and OSS, and remained classified to this day.

Faded and yellowed photos too of the dashing, Nordic-looking Linus Aalborg, muscular arms folded, standing by a cliff, in hand-to-hand combat training, and receiving a medals from Churchill and Ike.

Obviously in awe of Mr. Aalborg's derring-do, Buck pointed at a picture of the great man standing smugly holding a pair of Lugers across his chest.

"A couple of Krauts weren't around any longer to explain to the quartermaster what happened to their standard-issue sidearms," Buck told me.

Buck was florid, jowly and cynical. Spike, on the other hand, was rail-thin and ghost-pale. His deep-set eyes could make the most hardened criminal avert his.

Spike gave me the willies. Fortunately, he wasn't around the office a lot. It was rumored that he was in the snare of reefer madness.

I reviewed the thin Barnwell file. Herbie wasn't dead yet, but nobody expected him to come out of the coma. He was a skid-row bum with Rudolph's red nose and prematurely gray hair. If he was inclined to lift a finger and find a job, he was too perennially juiced to get even Christmastime Santa work. No parent in his or her right mind would deposit a child with a wish list on Herbie's lap and risk having their precious tyke topple over with him as he passed out.

The Aalborg Detective Agency was located in Herbie Barnwell country, a second-floor walkup on the south edge of downtown Seattle, nudging Skid Row.

It was above a pool hall, across the street from a finance company, and between a long-vacant building with a faded UPTOWN DRY GOODS on a side and a pawnshop that asked no questions.

The agency itself was appropriately seedy for clients whose knowledge of private eyes began and ended with TV and the movies and detective novels. The floors creaked and an inversion layer of tobacco smoke clung to the ceiling. Fluorescent lighting cast a yellowish, hepatitic complexion on those beneath it.

The Aalborg Agency employed a dozen agents, the majority stogie-chomping ex-cops and a miscellany of others with vague backgrounds who were hired because of connections that permitted them to get to the bottom of things.

I was their token "young college-boy professional", a callow youth available to run shady errands for the bosses and to sit down with prospective clients uncomfortable with the living, breathing stereotypes. If a prospective client came in wanting something done that they felt was "aboveboard", I was their boy.

I had a dubious family background which I will reveal in detail later. It was not a hiring impediment, however. All Buck and Spike cared about was that I had no outstanding arrest warrants.

We all wore modest business suits, although mine were clean and pressed. A lanky pencil-neck, I sported large-frame glasses with wide rims. The specs gave me a passing resemblance to Buddy Holly (so I'd been told), which I didn't mind at all.

My background as well as my appearance set me apart from my colleagues. I was a college graduate, in English of all things. That alone made me an object of ridicule. Furthermore, if I needed anything else working against me, I was a light drinker and non-smoker too, even the new filter-tip cigarettes the seasoned agents thought were for sissies.

Worse, far worse, was one of my two greatest

secrets — my virginity. If my sexual innocence had become known, the guys would've forced a couple of shots of cheap whiskey down my gullet, then hauled me down the street to a cathouse (operating under police protection) above a bar and a ptomaine parlor and bought me a $3 quickie on a filthy bunk with a blubbery, mustachioed female who did her nails as we coupled.

Marge worked the front desk and had the final say in assigning cases. She had been with Aalborg longer than I had been alive. She wore pleated skirts, false eyelashes the size of whisk brooms, and a Which-Twin-has-the-Toni home permanent. If the crew knew details of Marge's private life, they weren't talking. There was a collection of wedding and engagement bands on seven of Marge's ten fingers; I thought of them as rings on a tree.

"Herbie Barnwell's niece is waiting in the conference room, kiddo," she said, cigarette dangling in the corner of her mouth. "She's a looker, but pay attention to the file, not her gams."

I scanned the folder before going in, very aware who Herbie Barnwell was: Boomer King's hapless stooge. The occurrence was in all the papers. Humpty/Herbie had sat atop a wall at Boomer King's car dealership during the filming of a commercial and had indeed taken a great fall, making an extremely hard landing.

King used Herbie Barnwell to star in his Humpty Dumpty commercials. Herbie got to be halfway famous playing Humpty and Boomer King, our local DeSoto-Plymouth dealer, became a celebrity who couldn't keep cars on his lot, he sold them so fast.

The police had written up Herbie's last fall as an accident, one of those idiotically inevitable mishaps that take place when you're constantly blotto. Per

Marge's note, the cops treated the incident so cavalierly that it offended Mr. Barnwell's niece, his only local relation. That's why she was here.

I shook hands with Darla Hogan and sat down. Darla might have been my age or a few years older, but I evaluated her as far older in other ways; I saw that worldliness in her beautiful green eyes. She had a slim figure and silken hair that matched Debbie Reynolds'. My palms were sweaty before the interview began.

"How did you pick us, Darla?"

"You were first agency listed in the Yellow Pages, Mr. Bates. Tell me about your founder, this mysterious Mr. Aalborg?"

"Well, he was quite a legendary figure."

"Is he still with the firm?"

"No he isn't and please call me Brick. From what I understand, Linus Aalborg joined up after Pearl Harbor, leaving the agency to serve his country. He was sent to Europe, captured, then escaped the Nazis and fought them as a guerrilla. He was part of a team that blew up the Germans' heavy water plant near Stockholm."

Darla Hogan smiled. "Sweden was neutral. Try again."

"Finland?"

"Nope. They battled the Soviets off and on during those years."

"Okay, Norway?"

"You're warmer. I'm a librarian, a library science major and history minor. Where is the heroic Linus Aalborg now? I couldn't find a single thing on him in our card catalog."

Darla disabused every prudish, old-maid librarian stereotype I ever harbored. My voice was growing hoarse. I said, "Well, I'm told he disappeared after a secret mission or passed away somewhere as a result of wartime injuries and torture by the SS. There are other theories that he may alive and rotting in an Iron Curtain prison."

"Those pictures of him receiving medals from Winston Churchill and General Eisenhower, don't they kind of look like trick photography?"

I hadn't looked at them that closely, as they were in Buck's and Spike's offices, on the walls behind their desks.

"Not to me," I said, trying to keep my voice even.

"How about this?" said a smirking Darla. "Whoever started Aalborg wanted to be the first detective agency listed in the Yellow Pages."

The old hands enjoyed hazing me. Had they pulled the wool over my eyes again, them and their legendary guerrilla fighter? That and his disturbing quotes. For all I knew now, they were pictures of Heinrich Himmler's nephew.

But verification one way or another would require me sneaking in after hours and examining the medal-award photos with a magnifying glass. I dared not. It could be like a small child learning that there was no Santa Claus.

Humiliated that this cynical possibility never occurred to me, my neck and cheeks on fire, I said, "Hmm. That makes sense. Conceivably. I'll have to look into it."

"I'm sorry if my theory disturbed you, Brick."

I shook my head. "No. It didn't. Not at all."

"Anyway, it doesn't matter. The *Aalborg* name and a call to your secretary sold me. Marge, is it?"

"Marge is one of a kind."

Darla looked around. "She is a hoot. Marge could sell refrigerators to Eskimos, and they'd buy them or else. You people have the right combination of deviousness, seediness, hard-boiled ambience, and low rates."

I knew that the agency billed my time at two-thirds that of the veteran agents, $9.25 per hour and my pay envelope reflected it. "Well, uh, thanks. I think."

"Humpty Dumpty," she said, shaking her head.

"Humpty Dumpty sat on a wall," I said.

"Humpty Dumpty had a great fall," she said.

"All the king's horses and all the king's men," I said.

"Couldn't put Humpty together again," she said, her voice cracking.

"A creation and integral character in Lewis Carroll's *Through the Looking Glass*," I said.

Her beautiful eyes were glazing. I reached for a tissue, but she'd already taken one from her purse.

I said, "I was an English major. The novel was covered in Lit 305, Children's Classics as Folk Literature," I went on, unsure if that disclosure worked in my favor or not. A fictional private eye's studies concentrated in the areas of illegal surveillance, female client seduction, jujitsu, and reckless use of his gat. He wouldn't be caught dead reading a book unless he used it to swing it and break a bad guy's nose.

Evidently my soft-boiled education didn't hurt. Darla replied by writing a retainer check.

Her eyes aflame, she stood and said, "Herbie was a drunk, the quintessential skeleton in our family closet. He mooched off all of us and got into our purses and wallets if we were careless and left them lying around when we were stupid enough to let him in our homes. But if his fall wasn't an accident, nobody has the right to try to kill the worthless fucking asshole. I want to know why he landed on boards that time, not hay that was always there to break his fall."

Girls didn't as a rule didn't talk dirty in 1957, not in the company of boys. If they did, they were tagged as loose, fit only as the property of greasers, habitués of drag strips.

But her profanity inflamed me.

Worthless *fucking asshole.*

"Oh, you're as red as a beet," she said. "I'm sorry for my dirty mouth. I lose control sometimes."

"Think nothing of it," I said. "These are, well, modern times."

To tell the truth, so much blood rushed from my head to a lower part of my anatomy that I was woozy.

"My profanity is a byproduct of having three older brothers, learning from them and proving I could take care of myself. I gave as good as I got," she said. "They live out of town, not too far away, in Tacoma, Bellingham and Centralia. Far enough, though, to make phony excuses why they have to leave Uncle Herbie to me, the snots."

I managed to stammer that I'd immediately begin on her case, making it my highest (and at the moment my only) priority.

I killed my first man by slashing him from ear to
ear.
As the Nazi gurgled his last, pumping out his life's
blood,
I wondered if I had done the right and moral
thing.
I decided I had. He was an SS colonel,
to whom human life meant less than nothing.

- Linus Aalborg

Chapter 2

Suddenly It's 1960

DRIVING FROM THE AGENCY in the pool car, I analyzed once more why I became a fledgling PI. There were several cogent reasons, plus others I'm sure that remain buried in my subconscious, the optimum place for them.

1. I had graduated from the University of Washington in June with the aforementioned BA in English. Seriously, what do you do with *that* sheepskin? It had a fraction of a fraction of the currency of a BS in engineering; the starting salary of a mechanical or aeronautical engineer at Boeing and other big companies was a fantastic $5300 per annum. My mother and older sis wanted me to apply for a teaching job. After being in school for 17 years including kindergarten, I wasn't too keen on standing up, facing the other way in a classroom for the remainder of my working life.

2. There were hints of an upcoming recession (the real thing did hit us from August 1957 to April 1958) and employers were tightening their belts. I had to choose a career posthaste.

3. The Aalborg Detective Agency was running an ad for an entry-level position requiring a college degree and no prior investigative experience. Why they took me over other "young professional" candidates is a mystery, for which I'm grateful. As I said, my Buddy Holly likeness may have swung it, a built-in appeal. Or there were no other candidates. Or the other candidates were repelled by what they saw,

fleeing the interview as quickly as they could.

4. Another reason that I hoped would stay buried.

I arrived at Boomer King Motors, the biggest De Soto-Plymouth dealership in three Pacific Northwest states and northern California. It covered an entire city block on the south side of town, close to the Boeing plants, and was chock-full of cars, new and used. They were shiny and clean, paint and chromium glistening, hoods up, helium balloons attached. Engines of the used cars had been steam-cleaned of all exterior defects.

The lines of vehicles seemed to stretch to the horizon. The newer used cars were in front. A number had hooded headlamps and Dagmars, the latter being dome-shaped bumper extensions. They were named for Dagmar, the busty model and TV actress who in a brief flash of fame had made the cover of *LIFE* magazine.

Those styling features were fading from fashion, prime examples of how automotive styling changed virtually overnight. "Planned obsolescence" was the official term; plummeting resale value was the reality.

I saw dust and heard heavy machinery in the distance, roughly a mile and a half away. The new Interstate Highway System construction was now underway in our neck of the woods, our north-south one due to open in the early-to-mid 1960s. These highways were going to be called "freeways".

Contracts had been signed and property bought. "Government extortion" was a term often heard, futile cries from homeowners who had lived in their houses through two or three generations, dating to the late-1800s. The homes were slated to become memories, ghosts buried beneath thick concrete.

Nearby, an old street lined with warehouses and machine shops was being plowed under to make way for progress. Cement was soon to be poured for onramps and off ramps. Freeways had no stop signs and traffic lights, thus the name. Ours, Interstate-5, was to be a mind-boggling six lanes, three in each direction.

An entrance and exit not a half-mile from here was in the plans, serving northbound and southbound freeway traffic. Boomer King DeSoto-Plymouth's tall rotating sign would be visible, a boon to the dealership that will perhaps compensate for the demise of Herbie Barnwell and the lucrative Humpty Dumpty commercials.

Of further benefit to Boomer King — as if any was needed — was the purchase of farmland and pasture in our county by rapacious housing developers. The days of our city and neighboring towns standing alone with unique identities were coming to an end. Thanks to the freeways and new surface streets and roads, we were to become joined by a suburban blur of cul-de-sacs inhabited by citizens whose only practical means of transportation was the automobile.

Before going into the showroom, I took a stroll around the property, waving off salesmen more times than I could count.

If you are of my vintage and lived in the Pacific Northwest, you will remember the TV commercials. Boomer had his body and fender shop build a fiberglass egg in sections. It was painted colorfully, like the nursery rhyme character Humpty Dumpty, with arm and leg holes for whatever chump they found to sit inside it. Namely and exclusively Herbie Barnwell.

There was an old brick wall behind the service department that was easily 14 feet high. It was all that remained of the original dealership founded by Boomer's father in the 1920s, when it was a

Hupmobile franchise. Directly under the wall was a grease pit they'd used to drive cars over to lube them from below.

For the commercials, the filming crew helped Herbie up a ladder — he'd most likely be stewed and none too steady — and assemble the egg around him.

They'd hustle down fast, so the camera could roll in case Herbie fell before he was supposed to. The pit was filled with straw and covered by a tarp. Herbie would land, the egg flying apart on impact.

Boomer King then hurried Johnny-on-the-spot to the dazed Herbie, looking sincerely into the camera, saying, "Humpty Dumpty sat on a wall. Humpty Dumpty had a great fall. All King's horsepower and all King's mechanics couldn't put Humpty together again. But, by golly, my friends, Boomer King can put a heckuva deal together for you on the new De Soto or Plymouth of your choice or a cream puff from our vast used car lot."

Et cetera.

They said Boomer was a marketing whiz, a pioneer. These days, some might call him a "visionary" from a past age. What he was was a crook. The instant you walked onto his lot, his salesmen pounced. You'd be lucky to escape in one piece unless you signed on the dotted line. Everybody knew Boomer was slippery. That didn't prevent him from selling cars hand over fist after the Humpty Dumpty commercials caught on.

I entered the showroom to rich aromas of plastic and automotive fluids. It was overpowering. The dimensions of a warehouse, the showroom had tall windows, indirect lighting, and a floor of faux marble.

The star of the show was the new 1957 Plymouth Fury, half a dozen of them angled here and there, with their dazzling colors and space-age styling, as if ready for takeoff into earth orbit.

The same '57 Fury advertising seen on TV and billboards was plastered to the walls and hanging on banners:

SUDDENLY IT'S 1960 > PLYMOUTH
WHO SAYS TOMORROW NEVER COMES?
YOU'RE LOOKING AT IT!
1960-NEW FLIGHT SWEEP STYLING
REVOLUTIONARY NEW TORSION-AIRE
RIDE
THE FABULOUS FURY 301 V-8 ENGINE
TOTAL CONTACT BRAKES
EXHILERATING SPORTS-CAR HANDLING

Giddy stuff.

How could anybody resist?

Every single car was listed as "ON SALE". The Furys were "BARGAIN PRICED" in the $2900 range. I didn't know if $2900 was a genuine bargain or not, but it was far too rich for my blood.

Boomer King Motors's office manager had a desk in an alcove by a stairway. Paperwork was stacked high beside an electric typewriter.

A placard identified her as PEGGY. A buxom platinum blonde, she was no kid and had some hard miles on her, but bursting out of an angora sweater, Peggy sure was a dish, her and *her* Dagmars.

Unsmiling, she handled my business card as if were radioactive.

"A private eye?"

"Yes ma'am."

"What's this about?"

"Herbie Barnwell."

"Who?"

Was she being disingenuous or truly ignorant?

"Humpty Dumpty. You know, who took a great

fall during a commercial filming," I said laconically, like Jack Webb on TV playing *Dragnet's* Sergeant Joe Friday.

"Oh, yeah, right. Him. The poor little boozehound. It was an accident, so why are you here?"

"He's still in a coma, condition unchanged," I said, testing her response.

"Yeah? That's too bad," she said, digging through her paperwork, emotionlessly. "What's it got to do with us? It's a crying shame, but like I said, it was an accident. The cops even said so. If you don't mind, Brock, I've got work piling up here."

I shivered inwardly. Peggy was one cold fish.

"It's Brick and I'd like to speak to Mr. Boomer King. I won't take much of his time."

"Mr. King is upstairs in his inner office on important business."

"That's okay. I can wait."

"I don't know when he'll be available."

"I can wait."

She flicked my card to the edge of her desk for me to retrieve. I left it there.

"It might be tomorrow before he's done up there," she said. "Or the next day. He's busy busy busy."

"I can come back."

"It's your time you'll be wasting."

"I have the time."

She looked up at me. "Do you carry a gun?"

"No."

"They do on TV."

"This is real life, ma'am," I said, though there were times since joining the agency when I wasn't certain of that.

"No gun, huh?"

Thankfully, the Aalborg Detective Agency didn't issue them to rookies. I shook my head.

Peggy shrugged and returned to her paperwork.

I decided to do a slow lap around the showroom, kicking a tire or two, and see where that led.

"I'm Ken Bolling, general sales manager. May I help you?"

I hadn't gotten 15 feet from Peggy. I smelled his cologne before he came up behind me and I saw him. It was strong enough to kill mosquitoes.

Age 40 or so, Ken Bolling was tall and lean, a slick-looking piece of work with a pencil moustache, a seersucker suit, and aviator sunglasses in his jacket pocket.

I gave him a business card and said, "I'm looking into the Herbie Barnwell incident."

He stared at me. "On your own?"

"No sir. We have a client."

"Who, if I may ask?"

"You may ask, Mr. Bolling, but I'm sorry, that's confidential."

"Have it your way. It sure was a tragedy," Ken Bolling said, tsk-tsking.

"It was. I'd like to retrace the chain of events if you don't mind, Mr. Bolling."

"Follow me. I'll show you all we know."

As he led me outside to the brick wall, I thought it peculiar that Ken Bolling was so forthcoming while Boomer King was incommunicado and Peggy wouldn't give me the time of day.

"By the way," Bolling said. "That '54 Ford you're driving, is it yours?"

Therefore, I deduced, Ken Bolling had been watching me and was taking advantage of my curiosity to make a sale. This attention had nothing to do with my case. Naive me.

"No. It's the agency's pool car."

"What's your own private vehicle?"

I was making so little money that I lived in a rooming house and drove a clunker with too many miles on it, taped-up seat covers, and a sooty exhaust. "A forty-nine Mercury."

"Coupe?"

"Sedan."

"Guitar and stove?"

"Excuse me?"

"Radio and heater."

"Stove, uh heater. No guitar."

"Whitewalls?"

"No."

Bolling frowned in deep thought or the appearance thereof.

"Look, man to man, we both know a car like that won't be a hot seller and we'll have to stick it in the back of the lot, but I can go, sight unseen, as high as two-hundred smackers trade-in on your Merc for a new Plymouth Fury, a demo with very few miles on it and an easy payment plan. A young fella like you, you're made for tailfins and a wraparound windshield, the look of the future."

I didn't reply.

"You got a steady gal?"

"Uh, no."

He leered and winked. "That'll change when you hop behind the wheel of that Fury. You'll have to beat the babes off with a stick."

Very few miles? As I heard tell, a used car Boomer King DeSoto-Plymouth hadn't rolled back the odometer on was so rare it belonged in the Smithsonian.

I changed the subject. "I guess it must hurt to be in a plastic egg and land from so high, regardless if you're landing on soft hay."

"Ol' Herbie never felt any pain, know what I

mean? He loved the job too. He lived the role. 'Call me Humpty', he'd say all over town to anyone who didn't cross the street when they saw him coming."

"How often did you shoot? The commercials look the same to me."

Ken Bolling made a face and shook his head at my lack of artistic observation. "You got what you call your nuances. Herbie'd be up on top of the wall, flailing his arms and legs and topple over, landing on his ass or back or on a side. Depending, I guess, on how loaded he was, or the wind direction, that's how he'd land. Boomer ran different one-time-only specials and incredible sale prices too. The cars sold like hotcakes."

"Was Mr. Barnwell your only Humpty Dumpty?"

"Uh huh." Bolling tapped the side of his noggin. "Nobody but Herbie was goofed up enough in the head to do it. He had a screw loose from the sauce, you know. Three days a week or so, he'd hitch a ride out here, set up the ladder, and sit on the wall."

"Sit on the wall?"

"Yeah, just sit, for no good reason. He'd sit up there and look around, like he was rehearsing to play Shakespeare, you know. I had to chase him away a couple of times. Mr. King personally had to also. The timing of his injury's crummy too for us. Downright rotten luck."

"Why?"

"We'd heard from reliable sources that *Confidential* and the *National Enquirer* were picking up on the Humpty Dumpty story. They were both gonna do a goofy angle, like he was the real Humpty Dumpty, a time traveler from when the nursery rhyme was written. Everybody knows it's pure bullshit but it'd draw folks onto the lot like flies onto honey."

"The report said Mr. Barnwell landed on

something other than the usual hay," I said. "How did that come to be?"

"We're remodeling the used car showroom across the alley there," Bolling said, pulling the tarp away, exposing a stack of plywood and lumber. "Our monthly Super Semiannual Everything Must Go Or Else Pre-owned Car Sale's was coming up and it wouldn't do for a buncha scrap to be lying around. Somebody must've ordered cleanup workers to get rid of the mess. Signals got crossed. They dumped it in the pit by mistake."

"When?"

"I believe it was the day before the accident. One day or two."

"Who were the cleanup guys?"

Ken Bolling shrugged and took a cigar from a shirt pocket. "Don't know. We hire the stiffs as day labor through some soup kitchen downtown and pay them in cash when we have to have manual labor done."

"Do you recall which soup kitchen, sir?"

"Don't remember the name, but it's down between an old warehouse and a tavern that makes the police blotter in the news."

I think I knew which one. Unsurprisingly, it wasn't far from the Aalborg Detective Agency.

"Mr. King likes to hire on the cheap?" I said, goading him.

Bolling bit off the end of the stogie, spit it out fairly close to my feet, lit up, and said, "Boomer's a peach of a guy. He's the finest human being it's ever been my privilege to meet as an automotive sales professional. Boomer wept openly when the rummy went *kersplat.*"

"*Kersplat?*"

Ken Bolling angled a hand downward. "Yeah, *kersplat.* How else would you put it?"

I didn't know, so I didn't answer.

"You can check at the TV station that filmed the commercial. It's maybe still on their kinescope."

"I will," I said.

Bolling blew a smoke ring in my direction and said, "Feel free. No skin off my ass. It's your time to waste."

Humpty Dumpty Goes Kersplat!

Climbing an icy, vertical cliff in the middle of the night, dagger clenched between my teeth, is unendurable, but preferable to losing my grip and tumbling into a rocky abyss.
- Linus Aalborg

Chapter 3

Margaret (Peggy) Jones Hardin Callahan

AS SOON AS THE KID DETECTIVE amscrayed off the lot, Peggy headed out to her car for a break. She drove a gray 1946 Chevy Stylemaster coupe with a driver's door that creaked when opened or closed, a cracked windshield section gone milky, a clutch on its last legs, and bald tires. All this talk about prosperity in America and its two-car families, what a sick joke.

Her hubby, Eddie Callahan, who made a damn good living as a tool-and-die maker ($2.87 per hour plus time-and-a-half for overtime), claimed it was all they could afford for her. While he drove a 1956 Pontiac Star Chief V-8 that still smelled like new-car. Eddie claimed that to make the payments on it, he had to work late more nights than she could believe.

Not after she found lipstick smears on his skivvies, the sneaky no-good bum. If she could afford to, she'd've kicked his lying ass out long ago.

Peggy turned on the radio. While it warmed up, she lit a Chesterfield, took a flask of Jim Beam from the glove box, had a snort, and studied the private eye's card:

Brick Bates
Private Investigator
The Aalborg Detective Agency
201 3rd Avenue, Room 201
MA 4-5892

Not located in the ritziest part of town, she knew. It wasn't where she'd want to be at night.

The kid private eye, he kinda looked like that rock and roll singer, whatshisname, the one with the big silly glasses. The name was on the tip of her tongue.

For some weird reason, the Bates kid damn near threw a fit when she asked if he carried a gun, like he was gonna soil his britches. She should've asked to see a badge.

Him asking in a pushy way to see Boomer regarding the rum-dum bum who toppled off the wall, what was that about? Was he being straight or not, or was it bogus? And who the hell cared one way or another?

What was that word? Misdirection. Yeah, misdirection. The little shit was playing her for a chump. There was more than met the eye.

Who'd hired the agency that sent out that boy, that was the $64,000 Question.

Was Boomer's wife, Agnes, onto him and her? A shriveled-up shrew with stringy hair and an unforgiving look on her face, whenever she popped in to see Boomer, she gave Peggy the stink eye. Making no bones about it, the icicle of a bitch.

Boomer, Mr. Innocent, said she gave dirty looks to any attractive female close to him, none of them with just cause. How she'd gotten cuz she couldn't stand what she saw in the mirror.

Mr. Pussy Hound was more like it. Who knows how many other gals the great Boomer King was dipping his wick into?

Or, then again, was Eddie checking up on her, the two-timing four-flusher she'd had the bad judgment to walk down the aisle with?

The radio came on: Pat Boone singing *Love Letters in the Sand.*

I could teach clean-cut Pat a few tricks between the sheets, she thought, as she had another belt of Beam.

Then there was Harry Hardin, her first hubby, a drunken crumb who liked to slap her around after he'd spent his unemployment check barhopping. Hiring a private eye to dig up dirt on her to recover assets the judge awarded her, was he? Assets that didn't amount to a hill of beans.

The man was nuts too, crazier than a shithouse rat. When his mother croaked, he'd spent the life insurance to have a bomb shelter put in the back yard of their house that was repossessed six months later, a week before she filed divorce papers on him. The Russians weren't gonna kill Harry Hardin with an H-bomb. He was gonna do it to himself, behind the wheel of his souped-up Ford, doing 90, three sheets to the wind.

Peggy lit a cigarette from the one she was smoking and tossed the butt out the window.

The next tune: Buddy Holly and *That'll Be the Day*.

That was him, she thought as she tuned out the static. The boy gumshoe wearing those thick glasses, he did kind of look like Holly.

Peggy Sue, one of Holly's gold records too.

The boy detective crooning that tune to her while she taught him the facts of life, oh boy, that was a picture. A picture she knew she'd not be seeing without the assistance of Mr. Beam.

Who'd sent this Brick Bates here and why?

Ken Bolling, who waltzed him around the lot? Plenty of people would like to have the full scoop on Kenny too.

Peggy wished now she hadn't given that Bates kid the cold shoulder. She wished she'd played along and picked his brain.

She knew how to play nice with a guy, smile, get in close to him, tease his weenie, and pry what she wanted out of him. She'd done it a million times.

But Peggy Jones Hardin Callahan too often regretted what she'd done and hadn't done. Where men were concerned, she didn't have the brains of a turnip.

Every day of the week it was some goddamn thing or another she'd live to regret.

The story of her life.

Chapter 4

Critical Condition

KERSPLAT, I THOUGHT, getting into the pool car. An inelegant way of putting it, but my mind's eye sure did draw a picture.

As I pressed the starter button and the engine reluctantly turned over, Bolling, with index fingers on his lips, whistled to me. I got out, ran back to him, and took a slip of paper. The name of the charity that supplied the day labor had come to helpful Ken Bolling.

"They're as dependable as any of them are," he said. "Given the caliber of the losers those places all are."

I stopped at the hospital first. It was on Seattle's First Hill, also known as Pill Hill for all the hospitals. The one Herbie was in qualified as a charity, as it reluctantly accepted patients with neither funds nor insurance.

Herbie Barnwell was in a paupers' wing with enough beds to be an Army barracks. Poor Herbie, Darla said, didn't know he had visitors any more than he knew that he had roommates. Half the beds were filled, half the patients asleep, the other half in chairs doing crossword puzzles or reading comic books. The wing smelled like an open medicine cabinet in a stinky bathroom.

Herbie was having a good night's sleep and then some. There were plenty of flowers in the room, stacked on a side of his bed, a result of his fame. Fans were paying homage to the dying celebrity and fading news story without having to get near him.

Shriveled inside more plaster than I'd ever seen in one place, it was obvious that Herbie was no kid, but doubtlessly years younger than he looked. He had crow's feet, wrinkles galore, bouquets of gin blossoms, and his Rudolph's red nose was a deep purple. I wouldn't be surprised if that schnoz glowed in the dark.

The tubes and hoses running in and out of him reminded me of the gear Bell X-2 rocket pilots wore when they zoomed along on the edge of space at three times the speed of sound.

A doctor was going down the line, looking at charts and chatting briefly with patients. When he got to us, I asked him how it looked for Herbie.

The doctor wore a stained white smock and a stethoscope around his neck. He had acne scarring and tired eyes. This ward of the hospital had to be the Siberia of medicine. I wondered if forceps sewn up inside a surgery was in his past.

"How's he doing, Doctor?" I said. "Aside from the obvious."

"The *obvious* is on the beam. Skull fracture, internal swelling, and a chart full of broken bones. The prognosis isn't hopeful. To put it in layman terms, condition critical. Even if he defies the odds and comes out of this one-hundred percent healthy, he's led such a dissipated life, he won't see age fifty."

Then he asked me who might be picking up Mr. Barnwell's bills.

"I'd try Boomer King," I said.

The doctor laughed bitterly. "Fat chance. They won't return calls from our business office, which doesn't surprise me a little bit, given what I personally know about him."

"Excuse me?"

"I bought a snazzy-looking '51 Chevy Bel Air hardtop for my son from Boomer King Motors. What's that word — detailing? They had detailed it all right, washing everything inside out and steam cleaning under the hood. You could eat off any part of that car.

"King and his sales staff acted like we were best friends. After the oil leak and the engine knock a week later, they forgot I existed. Now we have a stained driveway and a car that won't run around the block without stalling."

The doctor and I ran out of things to say, and Herbie wasn't in a talkative mood either. I was leaving when I met Darla coming in.

She told me she's been taking time off at the library and had been here nearly nonstop and had just been out for a meal.

I'd've fallen for her like a ton of bricks right then and there, if I hadn't when we first met, her and her green eyes and Debbie Reynolds figure. You can have your Dagmars.

"Anything new on the investigation?" she asked.

Kersplat.

"I'm following up on some leads."

"Like what?"

I tried to sound professional and mysterious. "Well, I've really just begun and there are too many puzzle parts missing to speculate and come to any conclusions yet."

"Are you coming around to my way of thinking that Herbie's fall wasn't accidental?"

If Darla had said the sun rose on the west, as a certified agent of the Aalborg Detective Agency, I'd have proven her right.

"I am, I absolutely am," I semi-lied. "I haven't ruled anything out. I don't want to get your hopes up too high, but I'm definitely moving in that area. One thing often leads to another in my profession and there are missing links I need to join."

"I *knew* the right man was on the case."

Her smile had me seeing spots.

I told her I was on my way to check out a tip. My legs were so wobbly that I had to hang on to the railing as I went down the stairs.

I won't deny that I have known many women who were alluring, exotic and intriguing. Women who were as deadly as they were desirable.

Alas, too many of them turned out to be a Mata Hari.

- Linus Aalborg

Chapter 5

Chances Are

DARLA HOGAN SAT BESIDE HER UNCLE Herbie Barnwell, dabbing his forehead and cheeks with a damp washcloth and stroking the arm on her side, careful to avoid a spaghetti of tubes and hoses, and the bags that dripped into them.

For some odd reason, *Chances Are*, the Johnny Mathis hit, played and replayed inside her head.

Oh, it was a romantic ballad, a boy-girl song, but she was inexplicably linking it to Uncle Herbie. What his *chances are*.

Johnny treated her to a solo performance inside her head:

Chances are 'cause I wear a silly grin
The moment you come into view
Chances are you think that I'm in love with you
Just because my composure sort of slips
The moment that your lips meet mine
Chances are you think my heart's your Valentine
In the magic of moonlight when I sigh, hold me close, dear
Chances are you believe the stars that fill the skies are in my eyes
Guess you feel you'll always be the one and only one for me
And if you think you could
Well, chances are your chances are awfully good
Chances are you believe the stars that fill the skies are in my eyes

*Guess you feel you'll always be the one and only
one for me
And if you think you could
Well, chances are your chances are awfully good
The chances are your chances are awfully good*

By all reports, Uncle Herbie's chances were awful, not awfully good. Slim to none. But Darla wasn't giving up on him.

Spending her savings (that were depleting fast, with no financial help whatsoever from relatives who did not give a damn) on a detective agency to prove what the police wouldn't or couldn't, that Uncle Herbie's accident was no accident, it was probably foolish, downright sappy. Darla had seen the man perhaps six times in her entire life.

After all, the Humpty Dumpty commercials were lining Boomer King's pockets. Why would he put an end to this bonanza and who else had a motive?

Boomer King cared only about money. That was a given. It was not likely that Uncle Herbie suddenly threatened his income in any way, shape or form.

But she had to find out for sure. Absolutely sure. The authorities had opened and closed their investigation in an eyeblink because he was an alcoholic transient, not a solid citizen. That was *not* right.

She didn't know if Boomer King had spent a day in college, but he had frat-rat emeritus written all over him. The independents that lived in dorms came in all sizes, shapes, intellects and personalities, but the fraternity boys rolled off an assembly line. The hollow laughs, the pipe smoking, the cardigan sweaters, the incessant drinking, their affluent and overindulgent parents.

When she was in college, she'd had experiences with men that were less than wonderful, the majority of them frat rats. It was her fault too. She'd attended fraternity parties, wild keggers where things got out of hand.

Young and naïve, she initially believed what the frat rats whispered in her ear, that their feelings for her transcended sex. All that won her was a reputation as an easy fuck.

One of the louses had the audacity to say that he could get serious about her if only she had tits.

That's when she wised up and slapped him silly with one of the *Playboy* magazines he left scattered around his room to prove how hip and urbane he was. She had him bleeding from his nose, upper lip, and an ear. Two days later, he claimed that Darla had given him tinnitus. She told him where to shove his tinnitus.

Those days and those sorry excuses for manhood were in her past.

Darla Hogan hadn't dated in two years.

Upward mobility, that was what she'd naively sought. Her father had been killed at Inchon and her late mother raised her and her older brothers on her salary as a bookkeeper in a music store. Darla had learned how to darn socks at a young age.

Of everyone in her family, Mother's disdain for Uncle Herbie was the most forgivable. Darla's mother could least afford her parasitic brother's company.

Her brothers all had excuses why they couldn't at least make an appearance. They did say to let them know when he died and when the funeral was. They'd try to attend. If they could get away.

Yeah, right.

Yesterday, in the visitors' lounge, waiting to see Uncle Herbie's doctor, she had thumbed through an insipid ladies' magazine that told robotic housewives what to cook, how to dress, how to live, how to think. If *think* was the correct word.

She'd read a submoronic article on "How to Keep Your Man". It warned against bad cooking, which would send him to disreputable saloons. If he was earning a nice income and wanted an expensive cut of steak, cook it for him and cook it right, serving it on a nice linen tablecloth.

Let him have fun now and then too, meaning without saying it that if he got a little on the side, don't be bitchy, live with it. If you can't, pink panties with lace and ruffles should bring him back into the fold. And never ever forget that your husband is the boss of you.

Darla Hogan tried to picture herself with an apron on, an automaton cooking and cleaning for her dreamboat husband, an unfaithful ex-frat boy who'd gone to seed and expected to be waited on hand and foot as he sat on his fat ass drinking beer and watching bowling on TV.

Fuck that.

She'd slapped the magazine on the table, on the verge of throwing up. Slapped it hard enough on the table to draw attention.

If Darla was destined to be a spinster, well, that wasn't the worst thing in the world. Was it? A number of her library coworkers were and they weren't losing any sleep over spinsterhood, over not having a gone-to-beer-fat spouse sharing their beds. They vacationed where they liked, not to some hunting lodge where their man shot helpless animals.

Brick Bates seemed different. Yes, their relationship was professional, but if early impressions were to be believed, he had more integrity than an entire fraternity house.

Chances Are.

Darla hummed the song as she dabbed her uncle's face.

Chapter 6

Hard Times

I DROVE INTO A RAGGED FRINGE of old downtown and parallel-parked between two junkers, yet again thankful that the wheels under me, decrepit as they were, had not come from Boomer King DeSoto-Plymouth. A mechanical failure hereabouts was bait on the hook for thieves and toughs.

This area made the Aalborg Detective Agency's neighborhood appear swanky in comparison, all Cadillacs and mink coats. I would not want to be here after sundown without a firearm within easy reach, an impossible contradiction. You see, that I was scared to death of guns was my second deep dark secret, nearly as shameful as my virginity. Fortunately, only the Aalborg partners, Buck and Spike, were permitted to "pack heat".

The combination flophouse and mission that had assigned day labor to Boomer King's dealership was located between a dormant warehouse and a tavern with steel bars fronting every piece of glass. Windswept garbage and newspapers had piled against a long-abandoned building across the street, a putrid berm of flotsam.

A simple wooden cross nailed above the mission door served as identification. Butcher paper taped to the inside of a window advertised beds: 59¢ PER NITE.

The price of a meal to go with the room, I assumed, was a sermon, because one was just wrapping up. The preacher, whose moniker was Snell, and his flock, seated on folding chairs, their heads bowed, said their amens.

While the guys chowed down on macaroni and cheese, I gave Reverend Snell a business card and asked about the laborers he dispatched to Boomer King Motors.

He led me into his office, an alcove in the barn-like mission.

A thin, graying man in his fifties or sixties, Snell paged through a ledger and said, "I heard through the grapevine. Is it true about Herbert Barnwell?"

"Yes sir."

Reverend Snell cocked a thumb toward the hungry faithful. "Herbie Barnwell is very much like the majority of men I see here. Not a bad person, but forlorn and enveloped in the snares of Demon Drink. How is he doing?"

I shook my head.

"I'll go by the hospital. We'll say a prayer for him here too."

I sensed an inner energy in this man. He'd need exceptional resolve to run a mission like this.

"It couldn't hurt," said I, a nonbeliever.

He pointed at a page. "Here they are. Bill Randall and Ray Helms."

"Are they in town?"

"I don't know. Another characteristic these men have in common is restlessness. No roots, no feeling of responsibility. They come and they go. If a man wants honest work, I'll try to place him with employers who call."

"Did you place Herbie Barnwell at Boomer King's?"

"No, and I thank the Lord I didn't. It was a mission up the street, another Herbie frequented. I'm praying for their people too."

"Any general opinions on Boomer King and his dealership?"

"I've seen those bizarre commercials. I wouldn't go near there. Poor Herbie. Even landing in hay must have been a painful jolt in that contraption, let alone on hard lumber."

"It was. What do you know about Randall and Helms, sir? Specifically."

"Next to zero. Are you suggesting they deliberately harmed Herbie?"

"I'm not suggesting anything," I said. "I'm trying to learn the whole story. How much is *next to zero,* Reverend?"

Reverend Snell said, "Well, they struck me as rough trade. The way they carried themselves, the way they talked, and their insecure swagger. They were tattooed too, a sure sign of trouble."

"Tattoos are?"

"Unless a man is in the Navy or is a merchant mariner, they certainly are. I'd be unsurprised if they had criminal backgrounds more serious than public drunkenness. They're probably riding the rails now, in the next time zone."

"Did they have a bone to pick with Herbie?"

"To my knowledge, they weren't even acquainted with him. Really, who cares enough about Herbert Barnwell to hire a private detective?"

"His niece," I said, unwilling to cite confidentiality to this man, despite it being a violation of Aalborg Detective Agency policy. I'd tell him anything he wanted to know.

"Is she close to him?"

"She hadn't been, but she is accepting responsibility, doing what she can."

"I'm gratified that somebody on this earth loves

poor Herbert. The niece must be a fine and caring person."

"She is, sir. Yes she is."

I requested that he contact me if Bill Randall and Ray Helms showed up. Reverend Snell said he would and added sadly, "Humpty Dumpty. A children's nursery rhyme twisted for profit. And worse."

I watch every episode of *Dragnet* I possibly can. In my best Jack Webb imitation, I said, "Humpty didn't come out too well in the rhyme either."

Chapter 7
Boomer King

ON DAYS LIKE TODAY when he wasn't attending Rotary and Chamber of Commerce luncheons, backslapping and shooting the shit with the city dads, civic-minded fella that he was, Boomer King ate lunch upstairs in his office, enjoying peace and quiet and privacy.

Those big shots, they wouldn't give him the time of day before he became famous with his legendary TV commercials. The phonies, they had held him at arm's length, saying all kinds of shit behind his back, crook this, swindler that, but they sure didn't mind his cash contributions to their goofball projects, like cleaning up city parks that'll just get dirty again. They'd changed their tune fast. Just like that, Boomer King wasn't a bad actor. He was a benefactor.

Yes sir, this was one of those rare times for peace and quiet and privacy. He had a lot of things on his mind. Agnes had packed him a ham and cheese sandwich that already looked stale. She had the knack. Agnes was sort of good in the kitchen when she felt like it, which wasn't regularly. That was about all she was good for.

What it boiled down to, she was jealous of him being a public figure, the toast of the town since the Humpty Dumpty commercials. Agnes had been suspicious of him for years too, bordering on paranoid, accusing him of getting some on the side.

So what if he was? She was a block of ice in the sack, and he was a good — no, a *great* provider — bringing home the bacon in spades. He didn't say a word to her when the bills came in from the department stores. He'd let her have a charge plate for every store in town, but was she grateful? Hell no, the frigid bitch wasn't.

He was entitled, goddamnit. A man such as himself, a prominent businessman, a television star, and a leading citizen, a pillar of the community, had stress on him like all get-out and he had a right to relieve it.

Boomer read a trade journal as he ate. There was a big article on the Japs, how they were gearing up their automotive production, aggressively pursuing export markets. He laughed at the picture of a '57 Toyota Toyapet. A tin can as ugly as sin, it'd fit in the trunk of one of his DeSotos. What were the little guys making those cars out of, like the joke went, American beer cans?

Clobbering Detroit like they did Pearl Harbor? Not a Chinaman's chance. Taking on the Big Three and smaller brands like Nash and Studebaker, you're nuts if you swallow that.

They'd be going against tough-ass dealers like him and his old man and his Hupmobile dealership, guys who had cars in their blood. Dad had sold Detroit iron till the very end, when he keeled over while handing the pen to some gink to sign on the dotted line and take possession of a used 1936 Chrysler Airflow that burned more oil than gas.

God bless him, Dad had had the service department put heavy-duty motor oil in the crankcase of that Chrysler to cut down on blue exhaust smoke from the worn-out engine. A car man to his final breath, Dad was.

Boomer wasn't often this reflective and philosophical. Giving this unspoken eulogy to the old man, who had his bad side too, especially when he was boozing. A mean drunk if there ever was one.

Boomer wouldn't mind expiring the way Dad did when the time came. That or in the saddle with a pneumatic blonde. It'd be fitting, wouldn't it? Like father, like son.

He finished his lunch with a solid belch, thinking that when Herbie Barnwell finally got around to croaking, he'd shell out for the biggest funeral and memorial service this end of town had ever seen. He'd martyr the brainless lush and do a super sale in his name. There'd be a line going into the showroom that stretched from the parking lot to the street. Boomer and his sales staff dressed in black to somberly greet everyone.

Yes sir, the first quarterly *Annual Herbie Barnwell Memorial Sale.* He'd wear all black in the commercials too, like an undertaker. This new color television science coming along, too bad it wasn't on the general market yet. In his usual outfits, he'd stand out great in blues and greens and yellows and reds for contrast, but color TV in every living room was a ways down the road.

Boomer headed downstairs to walk the floor, to keep his hand in. He'd greet prospects and autograph brochures for them. The rubes loved it.

Peggy was at her desk, shuffling paper. He could tell when she was pretending to work, but doing nothing. He knew it gave her a reason not to look at him, obviously pissed off at him again for no good reason, just like Agnes. He didn't understand dames and their moods, and wouldn't in a million years. They could be as mysterious as UFO aliens.

Boomer caught a whiff of the liquor on her breath as he went by. He'd have to talk to her about it, tell her to switch to vodka and chew gum afterward if she really had to have a lunchtime pop.

But not now. An old boy with a big gut and suspenders had his eyes on a 1957 Plymouth station wagon, the Custom Suburban model, a blue-and-white two-door. Perfect to haul his five kids around in and take his 250-pound bride to the square dance.

Fresh off the farm, Boomer King thought; he'd handle him in person, make the hayseed's day.

Boomer was a big man with a looming, domineering presence.

"Hey, how're doing, friend?" he said, going to him with a wide grin and an extended hand. "Hi. I'm Boomer King, at your service."

Chapter 8

A New Wrinkle

THE TELEVISION STATION THAT RAN Boomer King's commercials I'd seen was the smallest of the four in town and the newest, the only one without a network affiliation, either ABC, CBS or NBC.

In Burien, a small city 10 miles south of Seattle, in a former hardware store that had gone bankrupt, the station sported more antennae on the roof than a NATO base. At the front desk, a counter where a cash register had once been, I asked the receptionist to see whoever was in charge of the Boomer King DeSoto-Plymouth advertising account.

"Mr. Joe Manning, station vice-president and senior advertising executive," she said, pointing me through a door into a studio that was hotter than Hades.

There were clunky cameras on dollies that easily weighed half a ton and blinding lights that were freestanding and mounted in the ceiling. The heat and recently added materials for partitions made the station look and smell like a lumberyard on fire.

I asked a skinny young guy with a cowlick who was pushing a broom where I could find Mr. Joe Manning.

"You're looking at him."

Television revenue for small stations was iffy, yes, but this was a shoestring operation and less. Mr. Joe Manning was not many years older than me. He was probably making barely enough to stay out of the poorhouse, the price of being on the ground floor of complex technical broadcasting.

I identified myself with a business card and said I was investigating the Herbie Barnwell fall.

"A terrible shame," Manning said. "I was there."

"Along with the cameraman?"

"I was the cameraman."

Should've known.

"Was anything different that day?"

"How so?"

"I don't know. You tell me."

"You're thinking somebody did it on purpose?"

"We haven't ruled it out," I said vaguely, with a lazy *Dragnet*-ish shrug.

"Who's *we*?"

"My client and myself."

"Who's your client?"

I shook my head. "Sorry. I'm not at liberty to say. Client confidentiality."

"Well, you and your client may be barking up the wrong tree. I filmed thirty or forty of these. Until Humpty — Herbert Barnwell hit the deck hard, they all went about the same."

"Who dreamed up the Humpty Dumpty idea?"

"Boomer King did. We'd made commercials for him before, Boomer walking around the cars and talking a mile a minute, pointing at prices sprayed on the windshields with shaving cream. Sales weren't what he'd've liked them to be. He'd been racking his brain to come up with more pizzazz. A new wrinkle."

"A new wrinkle," I said, neither a statement nor a question.

"Boomer said Humpty Dumpty dawned on him one day when he was out looking at that old brick wall, wondering whether he should tear it down and pave over the area to expand his used car lot. Think what you like of King, the guy is creative. He has a wild imagination. When it came to raking in dough, this guy has foresight."

Thinking of television in general and the 17-inch Raytheon in my room and the rabbit ears I had to turn just so to be rid of the snow and have a semi-clear picture with ghosts, I said, "Philo Farnsworth is credited with inventing the television system in use."

"Is that right?"

"I took a class in modern American history. Farnsworth fought a losing battle over patents and died broke, an embittered drunk."

Joe Manning looked at me.

Enough academic exhibitionism, I thought; an affectation I'd have to put a lid on. There was no room at the Aalborg Detective Agency for a pseudointellectual. I got back on track. "Do other stations do his spots?"

"Nope. We have the exclusive."

"On contract?"

"Nah, a handshake. We're by far the cheapest in town. Humpty Dumpty was going to be a one-shot deal, but it became instantly popular. We refilmed so Boomer could feature other cars he had for sale at the time. He loved performing in front of the camera too."

"Do you think a handshake will keep Boomer King with you now that he's a star?"

"Doggone good question. To tell you the truth, if the network affiliates are kissing his behind and he dumped us five minutes from now, I wouldn't faint from the shock. With Herbie Barnwell out of commission, though. Boomer might be recruiting another drunk to play Humpty or cooking up a new campaign. He's not saying."

I didn't nose into the money paid, which Manning would've told me was none of my business anyway. Boomer King paying the station what he wanted to and if they didn't like it he'd walk, that was my guess. Chicken feed.

I asked if we could watch a few spots, the last and two or three, for comparison.

"Why? The cops said it was an accident and that's that."

I hesitated saying that I was searching for overlooked clues. Vital Mystery Clues. If I spouted detective jargon, he'd be asking to see my gun and badge. And probably give me a hard time because I wasn't wearing a trench coat and fedora. Private eye series were almost as popular as Westerns.

"Just curious."

Manning took me to a movie projector mounted on a tripod. To show me how kinescope worked.

"How we do it with the equipment we have, first we shoot on 16-millimeter film, like you do making a movie. When it comes time to run the commercial, we project the film onto a screen and aim our TV camera at it.

"I read the popular science and technical advancement magazines on the newsstand. Someday they'll be able to shoot at the scene with a tape recorder gizmo. It'll be transmitted through the air and instantly processed. They can hook into the studio system and telecast it at the flick of a switch."

I nodded politely. Sure, I thought. That'll come when we can fly to the moon the way Buck Rogers does in the Sunday funnies and when computers are tiny, like the size of a dishwasher, and for sale to homeowners at an affordable price.

I watched the commercials until Joe Manning's heavy sighs suggested that he was thoroughly sick of rewinding film. I used to think they were funny. Used to. Herbie'd sit up there in that egg, big eyes and stupid smile painted on it, flapping spindly arms and legs that stuck out the holes.

Then go *kersplat.*

I didn't know Boomer King's given name. Presumably, his loud, resonant voice had earned him the Boomer label. He was a big, husky guy around 50 with a jack o'-lantern grin. In black-and-white, his face was a deep gray from a year-round tan they say he cultivated at his Acapulco vacation home. According to *Confidential,* the biggest of the big fly in to the Mexican coastal city to play. Rumors had it that Boomer hobnobbed with stars like Fred Sinatra, Liz Taylor, and Errol Flynn.

Boomer mugged for the camera and made his hands into a megaphone and yelled for Humpty to be careful. That was Herbie's cue to accidentally-on-purpose fall. He'd make a hellacious racket hitting that tarp as the plastic egg flew apart. Whatever he landed on, it had to've smarted. I'd want to be soused too.

I looked for patterns and didn't see any. The obvious difference on the last shot was that Herbie didn't move and Boomer King didn't begin his spiel. He just stared at Herbie, speechless, a rarity.

Then the screen went blank.

"It didn't seem proper to continue shooting," Manning said. "We had a medical emergency."

"What did Boomer do?"

"King brushed by me and went back into his showroom. He didn't say a word. I didn't know if he was going to call for an ambulance, so I ran across the street to a pay phone, to make sure it was done."

"Do you know if King did call for one?"

"I don't think so. When the ambulance arrived along with a police car, he came back out. When they had Barnwell on a stretcher, I overheard him tell a cop that he thought Barnwell had passed out. He said he didn't know he was hurt."

"Did King weep openly?"

Joe Manning looked at me, making a face like I'd told a sick morbid joke. "Not that I noticed."

Among the first things you're taught in commando training is that when you set a timer on a bomb, you leave smartly.
If somebody's in your way, you don't say "excuse me".
                                        - Linus Aalborg

Chapter 9

My Mentor (or else)

I'D BARELY WALKED INTO THE AGENCY when Marge waved a message slip at me. It was from Reverend Snell. Ray Helms had been in the city pokey all along, right under our noses. Helms had used his one phone call to tell the Reverend that he had information on the wino who fell off the wall in the plastic egg, and that he'd sing for a price.

I clicked my heels. "Hot dog!"

"Watch your language around a lady," Marge said.

"Sorry," I said. "Did you read this?"

"I did. That jailbird piece of dog shit's your clue to break the case wide open, huh? Your Vital Mystery Clue."

She was having fun with me, not a new phenomenon at the Aalborg Detective Agency.

I didn't reply.

"Before you charge out of here to solve the crime of the century, Buck wants to see you. ASAP."

Buck, along with Spike, had private offices in the rear. I was coming to think of Buck as a mentor, as well as my boss, a seasoned veteran who was patiently showing me the ropes. Thank goodness, Spike was nowhere to be seen.

I knocked.

He ushered me in with a distracted grunt.

Buck's office was all business: mismatched army-surplus furniture, dented filing cabinets, and a swivel chair that sounded like a tortured cat when it moved. There were no photos or anything else of a personal nature on his desk, only a heaping ashtray, and scattered papers and pencils. And of course, directly behind him, photos of the great Linus Aalborg having medals pinned on him by Churchill and Ike.

Buck was the epitome of the living, breathing PI stereotype. He had a hazy law enforcement history and had resigned (or was forced to resign) short of minimum retirement age. I attributed Buck's dyspeptic moods to bitterness toward that police department and society on the whole. He was a pessimist's pessimist.

I had no trouble locating and settling onto the chair as I could not look directly at Buck. His jacket was off. By their own rule, Buck and Spike were the only two agents permitted to "pack heat", and packing heat he was — a Colt .45 service model automatic, gunmetal blue with pearl handle grips in his shoulder holster.

It was the size of a cannon.

I know, I know, my fear of firearms is irrational, a phobia as baseless as a fear of clowns (I've been to the circus, so far, so good) and spiders. I was born and raised in a humane (albeit tragic) household. I was not deprived or abused. There were no firearms in the house (I wrongly believed). I have not been a shooting victim, nor have I witnessed same. I haven't served in the military, nor have I gotten a draft notice (my fingers are crossed) yet.

"Bates, yoo-hoo, are you here?"

As I looked at Buck, I fuzzed my eyes to take his gigantic shooting iron out of focus.

"Sorry, sir. My mind was on the Barnwell case."

"Your eyes are funny. You hungover?"

I lied and said I was, tossing in a sighing groan for good measure, knowing that it would please him. Alcohol abuse was no sin at the Aalborg. For me, it might be regarded as a rite of passage. I was maturing the proper way.

"I forgot to take aspirin when I rolled out of the sack."

Buck almost smiled, then offered me a Camel. I shook my head and he lit one.

"Marge says you have some developments on your rum-dum case."

"I do. A phone message from — "

"I read it too. Nice work, Bates. I called you in to remind you that we work for the client. We ain't the law. We go as far as the client wants us to go. If we got us a felony situation, we dump it on the police and let them take over. This asshole, if he'll tell you things he won't to the law, good. You're all ears. Got it?"

Aalborg Agency mentoring was direct, with no room for misinterpretation.

"Yes sir."

"Marshal Dillon on *Gunsmoke*, he blows away the bad guys. Me and you, we don't get paid to and we sure as hell don't get paid to be shot at."

I was in total agreement. Guns on television are okay. Every other program was a Western and a slew of them were scheduled to premiere in the fall. Good guys and bad guys alike carried guns and used them. If my phobia extended to TV, I'd have to lug my set out into the garbage.

"Yes sir."

"You're catching my drift?"

"I am."

"If Helms wants to deal, you tell the dumb shit, he doesn't deal with you."

"No sir."

Buck spit out a piece of tobacco and licked his lips. "Your client, that little gal Hogan, she's easy on the eyes, ain't she?"

Darla. A squadron of butterflies launched in my stomach. I'd take the case as far as she wanted and beyond, and suffer the consequences later.

I cocked my head and shrugged nonchalantly, nearly falling out of the chair. "Yeah. Come to mention it, she's not too bad. Not too bad at all."

Buck winked. "Client relationships are what you want to make of them, so long as we get paid. This little gal, the way I size her up, she's been around the block a time or two, so it's entirely up to you."

I resisted leaping to my feet to defend Darla's honor.

Buck picked up the phone. "You learn what you can from that scumbag Helms and pass it along to the dicks, and send the little lady a final bill. The cops will decide if it's worth reopening the case."

"I will."

"I know people who work at the slammer. One guy's an old buddy. I'll get you in without any hassle."

"Hey, thanks."

"Keep us posted, Bates."

Translation: So I could be tightly supervised.

"Yes sir."

"And, hey, don't take all year wrapping this up. We're letting you ride this pony exclusive-like on account of the little gal's checks ain't bouncing, but Marge has got files piling up we need handled. Penny-ante stuff."

Which I knew to be one spouse or the other ignoring their sacred vows of marriage. I dug up what I could on the monetary end and handed the file over to a senior agent for the voyeurism aspect and wrap-up.

Buck came across loud and clear.

"Oh yeah," he said, giving me a small envelope. "Here, drop this off you-know-where."

I walked out the door, knowing where. The shady errands for the bosses? This was one.

This isn't a morality play. This is war.
The Nazi is Godless and bestial, a rabid animal.
People live and people die.

- Linus Aalborg

Chapter 10

The Slammer

YOU-KNOW-WHERE WAS THE DUGOUT TAVERN on First Avenue, a quarter mile or so, too far south to see the city skyline. The Dugout had opened during Prohibition. Nothing much had changed since then, other than that they no longer sell bathtub gin out the alley door. The neighborhood was a slight notch up from the agency's. There was a Studebaker dealer across the street and a Flying A gas station next to the tavern, on a corner, and an upholstery shop on the other side that was currently advertising a sale on Naugahyde seat covers.

It was a warm day, so the Dugout's front door was propped open. Behind the bar and a wall of cigarette smoke was a blackboard filled with baseball scores, games completed and in progress. A radio with a game on played loudly as the bartender updated a score with chalk and his bar rag.

"From Buck," I said.

He took the envelope and said, "Sorry, nothing to take back to him. But he knows that. Tell him, he gotta lay off the Stars. They're good but they ain't gonna beat out the Seals and the Mounties."

I said that I would, although I did not dare. I don't know how much cash was in the envelope or which team Buck had picked, but I'd heard him and Spike argue the merits of the Hollywood Stars of the Pacific Coast League. Their superiority or inferiority to the San Francisco Seals and/or the Vancouver Mounties was of no interest to me, a baseball non-fan. They talked ceaselessly about the rumors that the Brooklyn Dodgers and New York Giants were moving out west. Also not my concern.

~ ~ ~

I headed back toward downtown.

The local jailhouse was part of the courthouse and not new. Fancy beaux-arts style on the outside and scarily ugly inside the jail section.

The linoleum bulged in places and the sickly-green walls were due for repainting. It was said that inmates grew old rapidly. The same could be said for their decor.

At the front desk, it occurred to me that *everybody* here carried guns. This was, well, a police station. Duh.

After the second try, I managed to stammer out the name of Buck's old buddy.

A detective named Clinton came out of the back. He was tall, lean and a bit hunched at the shoulders and neck, a praying mantis configuration.

In a hurry, he escorted me to an inner sanctum of hallways and locked doors. On the way, Detective Clinton told me that Raymond Helms had a sheet as long as his arm, mostly petty stuff. Two nights ago, a cruiser nabbed him behind a hi-fi store, coming out with an armload of transistor radios. He knew that our judges were tired of seeing his ugly puss. They were going to throw the book at Helms when his arraignment came up next week and he knew it.

As he turned me loose, he asked, "How's Buck hanging in there?"

"The agency seems to be doing well for him and the rest of us," I said.

With a combination of a smile and a grimace, Clinton said, "I don't know of too many guys who haven't reached into the cookie jar, but if you do with both hands, they tend to get stuck."

I said nothing.

"Give Buck my best wishes and tell him I said to try to keep his nose clean."

One mystery solved today, one to go.

Beyond the front desk and processing area, the place stank like the Black Hole of Calcutta. Strange animal sounds emanated from farther within, noises I had previously heard only in nature travelogues. A uniformed jailer with a key ring that had to weigh five pounds escorted me to a small room. In it was a steel table, a 1000-watt reading lamp, two chairs, and Ray Helms.

Helms, in his twenties, was a classic juvenile delinquent who graduated from stealing hubcaps to car theft and burglary. He was a scrawny punk with a greasy ducktail and mean, dumb eyes.

His arms were covered with tattoos: a heart with an arrow through it with a smudged woman's name he'd apparently tried to cross out with a subsequent tattoo, a sailing ship that looked like it had struck an iceberg, and someone's idea of a bathing beauty. I was now a firm believer in Reverend Snell's tattoo theory.

I knew the Ray Helms type from high school. Before dropping out, they considered remedial wood shop as an academic class. If a "teach" had the effrontery to ask them to open a book, they were being picked upon, and the "teach" was soon to be a victim of a flat tire in the faculty lot.

I had no solid plan how I was going to conduct this interview, so I let Helms rant and rave about his rotten childhood and lifetime of bad luck. How he couldn't catch a break. How the fuzz had it in for him.

I immediately overstepped my authority and reneged on assurances given during Buck's mentoring/lecture by cutting him off in mid-tirade.

"Look, I don't care who ratted you out to save their own neck on that fifty-one Ford you broke into last year or the teacher who blamed you for rifling her desk for test answers or the cat you set on fire in the third grade. This is strictly between you, me and my client, Helms. What do you have to trade?"

That settled him down. "What's in it for me?"

"Depends on what you have," I semi-snarled, emboldened by the close proximity of guards. "They let you out, Raymond, it's like you're caught in a turnstile at the A&P. The powers that be, they're fed up. They think you need ten years upstate stamping license plates."

"For a coupla crummy radios?"

I glanced at my watch and continued the hardboiled lingo that popped into my head out of nowhere. I was Bogie, doing it for Darla, my Bacall.

"Fine. Play hard to get, Helms. You ain't the only number on my dance card."

"Okay, okay, what it was, see, me and this guy, Bill Randall, a guy I run into riding the rails, me and him, we were doing some tear-out work at this car dealership. We didn't have two nickels to rub together, so we took this day labor job.

"We was almost done for the day when the owner took us aside. You must of seen him. He does them Humpty Dumpty commercials on television. He's famous. King. Boomer King I think it is."

"I may have seen him," I said casually. "The name sounds kind of familiar."

"Mr. King, he said to load as much scrap as we can find nearby into this pit. Until it's full. He slipped us each an extra fiver and said this is for working fast, don't be seen, scramming when we was done, and keeping our yaps buttoned."

"Did he say why the rush or the secrecy?"

62

"Secrecy?"

"Telling you not to be seen."

"Oh yeah. He's the boss, you know. He didn't have to tell us nothing."

"Didn't you wonder?"

"Nah. Not till I heard on the radio the dumb cluck inside the egg fell off the wall and smacked hisself cuckoo."

"Weren't you suspicious?"

"Suspicious of what?"

"Suspicious that it was no accident."

"It wasn't none of my business."

"You're unbelievable, Helms. Where's Bill Randall?"

"Don't know. Him and me, we drank up the money the same night. I haven't seen him again."

"Did you know the guy inside the egg, Herbie Barnwell?"

"No."

"Positive?"

"Word of honor."

Simply because he was too stupid to dream up a story like this himself, I gauged him as telling the truth and stood up.

"You gonna try to fix it for me now with the fuzz?"

I lied, saying that I'd go to bat for him if his story panned out, using all the influence I had. Not a complete lie as I had no influence whatsoever with anybody.

Outside, I stood by the car. I couldn't breathe in enough fresh air.

And couldn't quit wondering why Ken Bolling had made this so easy for me, a rookie at the Aalborg Detective Agency to, as Marge derisively said, uncover a Vital Mystery Clue.

Chapter 11

My Humble Abode

IT WAS GETTING LATE, so I knocked off for the day. The Aalborg had no time clock; the clients' needs and demands set an agent's hours. Us agents were paid a percentage of the fees we generated, in my case a pittance.

I ate dinner at a drive-in two blocks from the rooming house on a main arterial as traffic zoomed by, eating in the car from a tray hooked to the driver side door. My burger and fries and cola were delivered by girls on roller skates. Some were younger than me, some older, the majority cute in their shorts outfits. I don't mind admitting that I had fantasies about them, roller skates and all.

To call my abode humble was a boast. It consisted of a crackerbox of a room, a rust-stained sink, a dresser so pocked with cigarette burns it looked as if it had smallpox, and a swaybacked bunk I'd purchased at an Army Navy store for $3.

The bathroom was down the hall. I was in luck; it was unoccupied. I was able to take a quick shower without interruption. There were times when Old Man Gibson, across the hall, monopolized it. He'd take a *LIFE* magazine in there and sit until he was able to do his business. My late Uncle Jerry, on my mother's side, had been like that. My mother said Uncle Jerry was over 50 and that it was a problem common to old age.

My mother, who lived alone. My mother, 10 miles from here, whom I didn't live with or talk about. By unspoken mutual agreement. We loved each other, but it was a complicated story.

My TV's picture was pretty good, with few waves and streaks. The sky was clear too; that was said to improve reception.

I wondered many times what TV would be like in the future, other than color and picture clarity. How big the screens would be, maybe as big as 30 inches.

In *I Love Lucy*, Lucy and Ricky slept in separate beds. The gossip magazines insinuated that they slept in separate beds too, but different separate beds. *The Adventures of Ozzie and Harriet* and *Leave it to Beaver* had home settings unfamiliar to myself or any friends I had growing up. On TV, disputes were settled without yelling and violence.

Three of my favorite shows were on tonight: *The Lone Ranger, The Bob Cummings Show* and *Dragnet*. They were on ABC, CBS and NBC respectively. A slight rotation of the rabbit ears from one show to the next focused each.

Bob Cummings was hilarious. A lady's man, on this episode, one of Bob's ex-girlfriends made life uncomfortable for him while he was wooing another. Complications I doubted I'd ever have.

With the help of Tonto, The Lone Ranger brought the bad guys to justice after the Long Ranger shot the guns out of their hands with his silver bullets, drawing not a drop of blood. A good trick.

Dragnet was my favorite show, period. By the time Sergeant Joe Friday and Officer Fred Smith were snapping the cuffs on the bad guy, my eyes were drooping.

Just the facts, ma'am.

I climbed into bed, atop a mattress that was half concrete, half feathers.

But I couldn't fall asleep, thinking of Darla Hogan.

My boner was so stiff it was painful. In my overheated mind, if I masturbated, I'd be cheating on her, so I kept my hands above my waist, arms tightly wrapped.

I hadn't an inkling how I'd proceed tomorrow, except that I'd find a way to invite Darla along.

Chapter 12

A Field Trip

 THINK I SLEPT. Maybe. Maybe not.

I did not have a dream, wet or otherwise.

I was up so early that I had free reign of the bathroom, in and out of there earlier than the other guys, those with "real jobs", riveting at Boeing, many at Plant Two on the new 707 jetliner.

As several had remarked to me in the rooming house, contemptuous of my age and wholesomeness, by definition, if you wore a suit and didn't carry a lunch pail, you did not have a "real job".

I avoided them all this morning, so nervous I that could not eat breakfast. I went into the office and checked for messages. As usual, there were none.

Buck was in early too.

He lumbered up to me and said, "How's it going, kid."

"Fine, sir."

He had liquor on his breath and no coat jacket. I looked at my desktop to avoid the howitzer in his shoulder holster.

"Any developments on the Humpty Dumpty thing?"

I told him of my interview of Ray Helms.

"You make it sound like he spilled his guts to you. You didn't play cops and robbers with him, did you?"

"No sir. Absolutely not," I lied. "He acted like he simply needed to get it off his chest. I had nothing to do with it."

"Which means shit. Guys like him, see, they don't

know what the truth is. He's conning you. To get ten days knocked off his sentence, he'd sell his own mother to a whorehouse."

He coughed and laughed. "Unless she's already working in one."

"That was my impression too, sir."

I stood, anxious to be gone before Marge arrived and assigned me new cases. "Well, I'd best be off."

"Remember what I said, Bates."

"I know, I know, sir. I'll keep you posted."

Buck had not given me an envelope to deliver to the Dugout Tavern bookies or ordered me to pick one up. The Hollywood Stars lost last night to the Seattle Rainiers, 6-2.

~ ~ ~

In 1957, there was one phone company. If you didn't like them, you could send smoke signals. I was not alone in hoping that would change someday. They did, however, provide a pay phone on every corner from here to Timbuktu. I dropped a nickel into the first one I came to. That is, after I dropped it on the ground twice, my hands sweaty from nerves.

"Darla, this is Brick. You know, Brick Bates. Private detective Bates from the Aalborg Agency, you know —"

"Don't be silly, Brick. I recognize your voice."

"You do?"

"I do."

"I'll admit, you know, that I don't have, you know, a clear plan, but I'd like to run around today and see how the situation plays out. You're invited to come along, you know. The agency won't, you know, charge you for my time."

"That's sweet and encouraging, Brick. Run around where?"

"Well, I'm not sure."

"I have time off coming at the library. I'll call in. Why don't you come by for a cup of coffee?"

"Sounds fine. Great, actually."

"We'll call it a field trip," she said.

A field trip, I thought after taking down her address. All we had to do was find a field. I did have an idea I'd run by her.

I hung up, having succeeded in my dippy, gutless way of asking for a date.

~ ~ ~

Darla lived on the east side of Lake Washington from Seattle, in Bellevue, a town that was relentlessly oozing into suburbia. Her two-story apartment building was a short walk from a shopping mall so new the paint was probably wet. These malls were sprouting up here, there and everywhere, giving you downtown without being downtown.

Her upstairs apartment had its own bedroom *and* bathroom. With decorations and photos on the wall, it looked homey. The kitchenette where she took me wasn't much smaller than my room. I casually and jealously scanned the wall photos before we sat, on the lookout for fiancés, bridegrooms, boyfriends, et cetera. There were several of older men with a family resemblance, hopefully brothers.

"You're looking for Uncle Herbie?"

"Uh, yeah. Yes I am."

"He's not there," she said. "The closest he came to be photographed was a family reunion we had when I was in high school. He was living in a flophouse in Chicago. My mother and my oldest brother wired him money for bus fare, money they couldn't afford. He didn't show. The money went into his mouth and directly to his liver, the worthless fucking asshole."

Worthless *fucking asshole.*

"So how's Herbie doing?"

"No change."

I told her of my interrogation (stressing that it was far more hard-boiled than an "interview", me flinging a chair against a wall, shaking a fist in his face, along those lines) of Ray Helms with the caveat that his type were pathological liars.

"His only motive is being sprung from the slammer," I said knowledgeably, then paraphrased Buck. "Guys like him, they don't know what the truth is. To get ten days knocked off his sentence, he'd sell his soul."

Darla's admiring nod and smile raised a mountain range of goose bumps on my arms.

We sipped our coffee and ate blueberry muffins fresh out of the oven.

"Our field trip," she said, letting it hang.

If I had my druthers, it'd be a romantic walk through a meadow, arms around each other's waist, searching for daisies, not Vital Mystery Clues.

We'd be carrying a blanket that we'd lay out and recline on and — stop stop stop!

"Well, for openers, Boomer King DeSoto-Plymouth, the scene of the alleged accident."

"You're reading my mind," she said. "But what can we expect to accomplish. No one there is talking."

"Whatever we accomplish, we accomplish," I said nonsensically.

Darla looked at me.

"Whatever we do, we do *not* sign on the dotted line."

~ ~ ~

On this early Friday morning, red-eyed (i.e. hungover) salesmen were in the lot, preparing for the weekend, lifting hoods, hanging helium balloons, wiping away windshield shaving cream that had streaked because of the morning's dew and spraying

72

on new low-low-low prices, which were higher, a standard Boomer King practice when anticipating larger numbers of bargain hunters.

We went into the showroom. Nobody was there. A lightweight jacket was hung up on a coat rack behind Peggy's chair, but there was no sign of her.

We went back outside and walked around, giving the salesmen a wide berth.

We stopped at the infamous brick wall.

Darla craned her neck upward and wiped away a tear. I wanted to comfort her with a hug, *any* physical contact, but chickened out.

I saw a ladder on the ground behind the brick wall. Probably used by Herbie when he'd go on up to rehearse his Humpty Dumpty role, his drunken thespian nuances.

Acting on a hunch, I picked up the ladder and leaned it against the wall.

"What are you doing, Brick?"

"Playing a hunch," I said out the corner of my mouth, the way I'd seen it done by Bogie and his kind.

It was the sort of instinctive hunch I couldn't articulate or even perceive until I acted it out, the kind of hunch that must have on occasion kept Linus Aalborg alive while fighting incredibly long odds against the Nazis.

"What hunch, Brick?"

Foot on the bottom rung, I said, "I want to see what Herbie Barnwell saw."

"Save me a seat," she said, following.

We carefully situated ourselves, and sat side-by-side, arms erotically touching each other's backs for support.

Seattle's skyline treated us to a glorious view. The Smith Tower, our tallest skyscraper was in plain view. Completed in 1914, it soared 42 stories and 522 feet into the air, it was the tallest building west of the Mississippi and fourth tallest in the world.

"L.C. Smith was the builder," I said to make conversation and not look down. "He made his money in guns and typewriters. The Smith Corona — "

But this wasn't the view my hunch sought. Darla was the first to verify it.

Twisting turned around as far as she safely could, she said, "Holy shit! Oh my fucking God!"

Startled, I clung to bricks and did the same. We had a vantage point like no other of Boomer King's upstairs office, which did not look at all like an office.

It had a wet bar and the biggest bed I'd seen outside of a Rock Hudson-Doris Day Hollywood bedroom farce.

We were not seeing movie stars in pajamas in a Technicolor film. We were seeing what would be a dirty movie, illegal in all 48 states.

A bare naked Peggy's legs and arms were wrapped around Boomer King as he thrusted.

To me, this was Sexual Intercourse 101. My sole prior experience had been in the dorm. A fellow student had thumbtacked a bed sheet to a wall and projected a grainy eight-millimeter flick that starred Mexicans and livestock. He had smuggled it into the country after a visit to Tijuana and charged us 50-cents each per viewing, later claiming that the revenue paid for his tuition. I'm sure it did, as the shows were standing room only.

I imagined Herbie Barnwell living out a Shakespearian rehearsal, as Ken Bolling sarcastically put it, that or as one of The Three Stooges.

And seeing this coupling.

And the illicit lovers seeing him.

I imagined there was a Mrs. Boomer King and a Mr. Peggy, neither of whom would approve.

Peggy now saw us, and began chattering and pounding on Boomer's shoulders.

Darla carefully started down the ladder.

She said, "Come along, Brick. I think we've worn out our welcome."

Chapter 13

Peggy

POUNDING ON BOOMER'S SHOULDERS, Peggy yelled, "Get off me, you overstuffed lummox. Now, goddamnit!"

"Can't. No. Not yet," he moaned, plunging even more violently.

Peggy went limp and slapped his blubbery backside.

"Make it snappy. We have us a problem."

Boomer finished with a groan, rolled off her without so much as a kiss, and reached for a cigarette.

"Jesus Christ, what the hell's this problem of yours now?"

A swinger who cared strictly about getting his rocks off, Peggy thought. Boomer King believed he was a match for Porfirio Rubirosa, one of the world's great lover-boy playboys. Mr. Suave's technique was Gynecologist quickly followed by Tire Pump.

On her side, facing away from him, she shook a cigarette out of her pack and jabbed it at the brick wall.

"I told you to tear it down how many times, that or use the blinds?"

"There's nobody there."

"They've skedaddled now, but we had company, lover boy. Up on the wall, just like your Humpty Dumpty drunk."

"Who?"

"A guy and a gal. I didn't recognize her. The guy, I'm pretty sure, is that kid private eye who was sticking his nose in here, into your business. Know what he's after?"

"I haven't the foggiest."

"Yeah, right."

"What's that supposed to mean, Peg?"

"You tell me."

Boomer got out of bed and scratched.

"Shit, if they saw us doing it, I'm in a jackpot."

"Brilliant deduction, Einstein. Get some clothes on, for Chrissake. And pull the damn blinds. Blinds that were your bright idea to leave open."

"I like to look at you bare-ass naked in the light of day, Peg. Is that a federal offense? And how the hell should I know somebody else would climb up there besides that drunken dummy?"

Okay, she did like the way he looked at her. She was no kid. Before she knew it, the days of guys of all ages looking at her the way they did, they'd be gone forever. But still.

"What do we do?" she asked.

"I have to think," Boomer said, sitting heavily on a side of the bed.

Peggy picked her bra and panties up from a bar stool, where Boomer had flung them when he'd ripped them off her.

"While you have your thinking cap on, Mr. Wizard. Get your pants on too. I'm tired of seeing your belly and your shlong."

Chapter 14

Playing It By Ear

DARLA AND I DECIDED TO PUT our heads together. Not literally, of course, to my regret.

We walked across the highway to a corner hash house, a hangout for insomniacs and early risers who consumed gallons of java.

In a booth, out of sight of the dealership, we browsed a sticky menu and the breakfast special: ham and eggs for 69 cents. Neither of us was hungry. We ordered coffee that was vastly inferior to Darla's.

"Should we call the police?" I said.

Darla said, "Brick, what do we tell them, that we're trespassers and voyeurs who spied a couple of legal age screwing? We didn't witness a crime. We may have committed one."

I knew for a fact that adultery was not a crime in our state as it was in a score of others. "Yeah, you're right."

We let our coffee grow cold.

I finally said, "Darla, let's go back there."

"And do what?"

I shrugged. "We'll be impromptu."

"Yes. We'll play it by ear."

"And look at cars. That's no crime either."

She smiled. "The only crime committed is by the salesmen if we sign on the dotted line."

~ ~ ~

When we entered the showroom, Boomer King was pacing the floor and Peggy sat at her desk, studying file folders, tallying numbers on her hand-

79

crank adding machine, pretending she didn't see or hear us. Her hair was askew and perfume was as potent as Ken Bolling's cologne. Mixed with perspiration, it was not pleasant.

Boomer King came to us, flashing his jack o'lantern grin, gave me a bone-crusher handshake, and said, "Hey, you're the private eye, aren't you?"

He knew by process of elimination, I thought. I presented my agency ID and badge. "I am."

Boomer held by ID card up to the light, as if it might be counterfeit.

"Brick Bates. Is being a shamus like it is in the movies? You know Sam Spade and them?" he said and laughed. "You kick ass, save the cops the trouble of solving the crime, and get the girl?"

He'd given me an opening. "On occasion it is, yes sir. We're doing our job and out of the blue we stumble upon a crime that we are instrumental in solving for the police and society at large."

Darla saw where I was going and fell into step. "I hired Mr. Bates to look into my Uncle Herbie Barnwell's fall from your wall, sir."

Boomer looked at Darla, and Peggy looked at Boomer.

"Say, great timing. I was just on my way to the hospital to visit my little pal. How's he doing?"

"Greatly improved. They say he's making a miraculous recovery," Darla bluffed. "I am *so* happy."

"Yeah," I said, catching on. "As a matter of fact, yesterday evening, he came out of his coma and told us some interesting things. It was hard for him to talk and we had to listen closely, but we got the general idea."

A large shadow fell over Boomer. "Yeah, like what general idea?"

Darla said, "You tell us, Mr. King. Uncle Herbie

didn't leave out one fucking detail regarding what he once saw on your wall. He said his eyes damn near popped out of his head."

Boomer wagged a finger at her. "Little lady, you have a mouth on you for a gal. I don't appreciate dirty, filthy language in my show —"

"I ain't taking any of the rap for this, Horace," Peggy shrieked.

Horace?

"I told you he wouldn't remember a fucking thing, what he saw us doing and say a word even if he did," Peggy went on. "But, oh no, Mr. Genius, you had to go and fix him by having those bums load up the grease pit with boards."

As Boomer ushered me aside with a cock of the head and a wink, Peggy broke into tears. Darla hurried to her, taking a tissue from her purse.

"You're a man of the world too, my friend," he said in a low voice, coaxing me along by my elbow as if we were square dance partners. "You know how dames can be. How they can get at that time of the month when they're riding the cotton pony, or for no reason at all their hormones get discombobulated and accuse you of something they make up out of the clear blue sky, especially when it's not going swell for 'em at home."

"No, I don't know, Mr. King."

"Call me Boomer, Brick. She's on her second husband and working up to her second divorce, you know. That tells you the story on her."

"It does?"

"Divorcees, they fuck like minks. That's a known fact, Brick. They can't get their fill of the ol' salami."

I nodded. Perhaps it was true. If anyone knew that for a fact, it was Horace Boomer King.

"Say, young man, just out of curiosity, what kind of car do you own?"

We were in my own car, not the agency pool car. "A forty-nine Mercury."

Boomer scratched his jowls in deep thought. "By golly, my friend, that make and model Merc is aging like fine wine. It's already a classic."

"It is?"

"Yessiree. They didn't manufacture very many of them. Take it from me, that's the clincheroo for classic-car stardom, that and styling that makes them look sleek and classy forever. It's a favorite of kids who hot-rod them too. It's got everything going for it."

"Uh huh," I said noncommittally.

"Come to mention it. I saw you drive in. At a glance, I'd say your Merc's in cherry condition."

Cherry? He sure wasn't looking at my car. That or he was farsighted and/or nearsighted. The only thing cherry about it was the driver.

I said nothing.

"I can swap you straight across for a brand new fifty-seven Plymouth Fury with dual pipes, radio and whitewalls, and owe you besides."

I didn't know what to say, so I said, "I'll have to think about it."

"Don't think too long. I already have a buyer chomping at the bit for the unit I have in mind."

"I'll have to think about it," I repeated.

"You drive a hard bargain. See that brand-spanking-new '57 DeSoto Adventurer ragtop in the center of the showroom? That's the one I'm talking about. There are gold accents on the grille, a hood ornament that's a work of art, and deluxe wheel covers. Rear-view mirrors. Big husky V8, with twin 4-barrel carbs. Three-hundred-and-forty-five horsepower. Push-button, three-speed, Torque-Flite automatic tranny. Power drum brakes, front *and* rear. Those dual exhaust pipes, you'll love that baritone sound. It's priced at over four grand. I won't let it out the door for a penny less."

"It is neat, that's for sure. Groovy."

"Cruise around town in that, Brick, and you'll get more ass than a toilet seat. Say the word and it's yours."

"I'll think about it."

"What do you say, pal? We have to wrap up the deal now. I got a prospect coming in later who's ready to sign the papers on it. Let's you and me beat him to the punch."

I had to get out of there and think.

The Aalborg Detective Agency did *not* take bribes. Not by fledgling agents anyway.

I gave Darla a jerky nod. Peggy was on her feet and they were hugging.

"I'll run home for the title to my car," I told Horace (Boomer) King.

Gary Alexander

The last man I knew who took a bribe from the Nazis
was paid in counterfeit currency.
And at the cost of his life, compliments of yours truly.
                                                    - Linus Aalborg

Chapter 15

Detective Harrison

MY INITIAL IMPULSE WAS TO GO BACK to the office with Darla to seek advice.

I vetoed that because:

1. I didn't want to subject her to leering and catcalls. The Aalborg Detective Agency was not known for its decorum and its attitude toward women was visceral.

2. The smoky atmosphere. Recently, doctors have been claiming that cigarettes cause cancer and heart attacks. I don't know if this is quackery or science, but while I'll take my chances, I'm not going to expose Darla to the risk.

3. I did not want to share her in *any* regard.

Instead, I invested a nickel in a telephone booth in front of the hash house and informed Buck of the entire series of events.

He said, "Looks like you brewed up a shitstorm, boy."

"Yes sir. It may have evolved into that."

"Evolved. A ten-dollar word that's a fucking understatement. Bates, you got the earmarks of an agent who ain't ever gonna stop stepping on his own pecker."

I had no reply to that.

"Your client's with you, you say?"

"Yes sir."

"She's happy with how the situation's going?"

"Yes sir."

"You ain't jumping her bones on company time, are you?"

I visualized a tallow-toothed grin. "No sir."

His sigh was a gravelly wheeze.

"I guess that's the important thing, so long's her checks don't bounce."

"They won't. They absolutely won't."

"Stay put. I'll get in touch with another detective I know from the olden days."

We waited by the phone for his return call. Dark clouds were obscuring the sun, so we moved under the awning of a five-and-dime next door.

"Peggy acts tough and brassy, but deep down in her heart an insecure and sweet lady," Darla said. "Men have taken advantage of her all her life. She's not a bad person."

I wasn't about to argue this with her. "No, she isn't."

"Do you think the police will implicate her?"

"I don't know," I said. "Another thing I don't know. Ken Bolling."

"That slimy sales manager you described?"

"Yeah. Where was he?"

Good question. We were puzzling over Bolling when the phone rang. Buck said not to go away.

"For how long?"

"Until my guy gets there," he said, before hanging up.

~ ~ ~

Half an hour later, an oxidized-blue 1951 Ford coupe pulled up. The uniformed driver and a plainclothesman got out. I don't know what I expected. The cop was average everything with a sidearm I could not identify because I rendered it out of focus.

However, the detective wasn't anyone I'd envisioned, Joe Friday or anyone else.

He was a Negro, a rarity within a rarity in the Pacific Northwest.

We are not in the Deep South, Birmingham or one of those places, thank goodness, where they burn crosses and inbred morons scream at Negro children as they try to attend schools of their choice. Label me a hypocrite if you wish, but it's just that Negroes are a minority in our populace, so they're simply a surprise in any context.

My mouth must have been hanging open, for he said, "Better close that pie hole or you're gonna be catching flies."

"You're a Negro."

"Been one as long as I can remember."

"I meant no offense, sir."

"None taken. Your boy Buck, he's a cracker too, but him and me, we're tight. After the scandal seven or eight years ago, where Buck and Spike and others got nabbed with their hands in the cookie jar, there was a void some of us in uniform filled with promotion to detective. You're probably too young to remember it. You were doing your arithmetic tables and dipping pigtails in inkwells."

That cookie jar again. Not at all like my mother's, with her homemade peanut butter.

I laughed, giving him his due.

He presented his badge and said, "Detective Harrison. Buck says Boomer King's up to no good."

There was a hint of a smirk, as if Boomer King and "up to no good" were synonyms, which, of course they were.

"Did Buck tell you what I told him?" I said.

"He did, but let's hear it from you."

Darla and I left nothing out.

"You say he bribed you with the most expensive car in his showroom?"

"He did."

"That'll be hard to make stick. It's his word

against yours. The Humpty Dumpty allegation, now that's something else altogether. Something we can get some teeth into."

"The *Herbert Barnwell* allegation," said his niece.

"Sorry," Detective Harrison said, averting his eyes from her icy stare.

He took a pair of walkie-talkies out of the trunk, switched them on so the vacuum tubes could warm up, and gave one to the police officer.

"All right, Bill here will stay outside the showroom and we'll go in and talk to this Peggy gal before she has a change of heart."

Peggy was at her desk.

Detective Harrison showed her his badge and said, "You have information on the Humpty — Barnwell fall I want to hear."

Unfortunately, Peggy had regained her composure. Boomer King and his charm had won the moment.

Refusing eye contact, she fluffed her hair and said, "You'll have to clear that with Mr. King. Anything I tell you too."

"Where is he?"

"Upstairs in his office, in conference."

Detective Harrison started up the stairs, us on his heels.

"Hey, you can't do that," Peggy yelled.

Maybe we couldn't, not legally, but we were doing *that*. I recalled from a Constitutional Law class that the Fourth Amendment addressed search warrants and that there were court decisions upholding it, but in a real-life situation, I presumed that Detective Harrison knew the law better than yours truly. I'd gotten a gentleman's C in the course too.

"Some office. Make some whoopee while you're doing the books," Harrison said as checked out the bed and bar.

He looked in the bathroom. "Nobody home there either."

Darla spotted a second doorway and set of stairs behind the wet bar.

She said, "I'll bet he's in conference outside."

On his walkie-talkie, speaking into loud static, Harrison said, "Bill, make tracks around the building and detain Mr. King if he comes out. We're on our way."

Harrison and I took the steps two at a time, our slipstream ruffling papers on Peggy's desk.

Darla brought up the rear and stayed with Peggy.

Bill and Boomer were in front of a red-and-white '57 Plymouth Fury with dual pipes. It looked hot. A soft suitcase was on the hood and Boomer was talking a mile a minute to the impassive Bill, whose hands were on his hips.

Boomer turned his attention to us as we approached.

"Somebody want to tell me what the fuck's going on? I'm a prominent businessman and leading citizen minding my own business. Business you have no right to interfere with."

Detective Harrison had his badge out again. Boomer looked at it and Harrison at least twice.

"Listen, I don't know what's going on, boy, but I know plenty of important people in this town. I know everybody who's anybody."

I saw that the "boy" didn't go over well with Detective Harrison. He stepped closer to Boomer and said, "Where are you going, Mr. King?"

"If it's any of your beeswax, I'm taking a vacation. If you listened to this private eye, you're way off base. That badge of his looks like it came out of a cereal box."

Offensive as that crack was, it wasn't far wrong, I had to admit.

"Where are you going on your vacation, Mr. King?"

"Acapulco. I bought Ava Gardner a drink once and went on a bender with Errol Flynn. Man, he can knock it down. His liver has got to be the size of Delaware."

Monumentally unimpressed, Detective Harrison said, "Before you leave to booze it up with ol' Errol, I need to ask you some questions about Herbert Barnwell's fall."

"Hey, I already have reservations."

"I know Mr. Flynn will be disappointed that you're late, but it can't be helped. Your secretary claims that Mr. Barnwell's fall and injuries wasn't an accident."

Boomer winked at him, going the man-to-man route again. "You know how ladies can be. When they're on the rag."

Detective Harrison replied with a stony stare.

He stood closer to the detective and said, "Listen, I know how you people love Cadillacs. I've got a cream puff out in the lot, a fifty-four Caddie Deville coupe that I'll let you have for a song. You'll be a real hepcat."

"Don't you try to bribe him and don't tell me how ladies can be, you lying sack of shit!" Peggy yelled from our rear. "You and all your promises. You were gonna blow town without me, weren't you? You guys check inside that bag the bastard has. If it's not full of money, I'm Groucho Marx."

Darla was in the doorway. Peggy was at her side, a lovely and reassuring hand on her arm.

"Hey."

Bill ignored Boomer's protest and opened the bag. Taped packets of $50 and $100 bills fell out.

"What do I get if I squeal on the slimy son of a bitch?" Peggy said. "I want immunity. I didn't do anything."

Detective Harrison said, "I'm not the DA or a judge, ma'am, but I know your cooperation will be looked upon favorably."

"You got yourself a deal, Detective," she said, middle digit aimed at Boomer. "I'm gonna sing like a canary!"

"She's hysterical," Boomer yelled. "You can't believe a word she says."

"Bill, cuff him."

"You can't do this! I got my Constitutional rights."

Whatever Boomer thought his Constitutional rights were, Bill could do *this* and did, spinning Boomer around and snapping on the handcuffs. Bill drove the squad car to us.

As they loaded Boomer into it, he bellowed at me, "I'll get you for this, Bates, you too, Peg, and that rummy, no matter how long it takes."

An empty threat.

So I believed.

I have a word of warning to every Quisling lackey
who sells out his country to the Nazis.
You mean nothing more to us resistance fighters
than a cockroach and will be treated as such.
                                            - Linus Aalborg

Chapter 16

Vinyl

EVERYBODY KNOWS THAT PHONOGRAPH RECORDS come in three speeds, roughly their revolutions per minute: 33, 45 and 78.

Thirty-threes and 78's are the same diameter, completely covering the turntable. Drop the needle on a 33 and switch the speed to 78, and Paul Robeson sounds like Donald Duck.

Thus, grandiloquently, that was how my small world moved in the next two weeks, sped up from 33 to 78, and as it sped by, not always coherently.

~ ~ ~

Margaret (Peggy) Jones Hardin Callahan went before a preliminary hearing and restated her willingness to testify against Horace N. (Boomer) King.

Raymond J. Helms was eager to take the stand too, though his testimony was regarded by the prosecutors as possibly doing more harm than good. He was unstable, his tattoos were visible, and his oath to tell the truth and nothing but the truth would be regarded by everyone as meaningless.

An APB on Bill Randall was fruitless; he was in the netherworld of bindle stiffs, making himself scarce without even trying.

Margaret (Peggy) Callahan was very persuasive and her testimony alone was deemed sufficient for the DA's case. Per the deal, she pled guilty to Accessory to Manslaughter and Withholding Evidence, and was given a 90-day suspended sentence.

The tabloids that had picked up the scent of Boomer's Humpty Dumpty shtick attended, as well as the legitimate press. Boomer also attracted a first-come-first-seated gallery. Flashbulbs from the Speed Graphics transformed the courtroom into the Fourth of July. Peggy was the hottest jurisprudential number to come along since Bugsy Siegel's Virginia Hill testified at the Kefauver hearings.

Accessorizing Margaret (Peggy) Jones Hardin Callahan's painted-on wardrobe was a single red rose, fresh daily. It was pinned on her in the courthouse hallway by Kenneth Bolling, sales manager at Boomer King DeSoto-Plymouth. Bolling didn't miss a minute of the proceedings, and didn't seem to mind flash bulbs in his face either, grinning broadly for one and all.

Those roses spoke volumes about Bolling. How he sprinkled Vital Mystery Clues for me as if bread crumbs. How he was conspicuously absent when the flap began at the showroom and Detective Harrison arrested Boomer King.

Darla told me that she thought Bolling was carrying a torch for Peggy the size of the Statue of Liberty's.

"I can't imagine what was going through the poor man's mind whenever she went upstairs with King," she said sympathetically.

~ ~ ~

Horace (Boomer) King and his lawyer, Logan Spliff, a notorious ambulance chaser and criminal mouthpiece, went before a preliminary hearing too. Stumpy, not young, with frizzy white hair that appeared to be styled with a finger in a light socket, and the complexion of a rotten beet, Spliff resembled every cartoon of a pinko or outright Commie lawyer I'd ever seen. Fact was, he was a personal friend of

Vice President Richard M. Nixon, so he packed some clout.

Buck and Spike had bitter stories about Logan Spliff when they were on the force, how he got his sleazy clients off with the flimsiest of excuses and technicalities. Making a phone call to someone with influence if need be.

Buck and Spike knew or knew of Boomer's daddy. They said the old man wasn't too big a crook for a car dealer and had to be rolling over in his grave.

After three days of preliminaries and jury selection, it all came down to a smoke-filled room, Spliff and the DA cut a deal. They had Boomer dead to rights, so he lacked leverage. Boomer pled down from Attempted Murder to Criminal Assault, anxious to be done with it before Herbie Barnwell checked out. He'd have to do 18 months.

But in the chain from deal to sentencing, there was a faulty link somewhere. I theorized that it was an unhappy Boomer King DeSoto-Plymouth customer, maybe Hizzoner himself. A faulty link that not even Logan Spliff could fix.

The gavel came down and Boomer got five years. Hard time in the big house, an institution populated by killers, bank robbers and dope fiends.

Boomer had to be restrained by bailiffs from attacking the bench. Logan Spliff threw a red-faced fit, but the judge gaveled them into silence.

There would be no bail for appeals or anything else; on the loose, he'd be in Acapulco in the blink of an eye. Boomer would indeed stay behind bars until Chrysler quit making DeSotos.

King's face was as red as a ripe tomato when they led him out. I thought he was giving me the evil eye, but it may have been Ken Bolling, who sat directly to my rear. And/or.

~ ~ ~

The afternoon of King's arrest, Darla had been called out of town for a maiden aunt's funeral and to aid in disposing of her estate and her dilapidated Victorian house, a physical and paperwork mess. For instance, she had seven cats.

To keep Darla filled in, we spoke on the phone every day. It cost me a small fortune in nickels, but did I give a hoot? Three guesses and the first two don't count.

From what I could read from Darla's tone, our chats were all business, but I rationalized it as stress.

I missed her like I have never missed another person.

Ever.

Chapter 17

H.N. King #73841

BOOMER KING WAS THE CITY JAIL'S latest celebrity guest. He had a cell to himself. Boomer preferred to stay in it and brood about the unfairness of life, away from riffraff, common criminals — a living, breathing art gallery of bad tattoos.

A book had been left in the cell. Boomer wasn't much of a reader, but this one caught his fancy. It was the biography of Reinhard Heydrich, a sweetheart of a Nazi. He was known as the Blond Beast, a nickname he richly earned by supervising the slaughter of Jews and other innocents. The book claimed that even Hitler was uneasy in the company of the Blond Beast.

Man oh man, Boomer could use the Blond Beast at the dealership as a closer.

Agnes visited him one time. She said the IRS had served her a subpoena. Their greedy eyes were on the dealership and their home. What should she do?

Boomer told her to insert the subpoena in a dark, warm place.

She never returned and he had no other visitors.

~ ~ ~

The Washington State Penitentiary was in the town of Walla Walla, in the southeastern corner of the state, an eight-hour drive from Seattle. It was in the midst of wheat fields and rattlesnakes, a highly unfriendly place surrounded by tall fence and barbed wire, and heavily-armed guards in towers, trigger fingers itching.

Shackled with other prisoners, he rode there in a

bus that had slits for windows. Treating him like a common criminal.

It was still daylight when they arrived at in-processing.

They hung a number with the day's date around his neck and snapped two photos as they had in the Seattle lock-up, facing ahead and profile, each expression smug and arrogant. They confiscated his personal belongings and gave him a receipt for them.

"My belt too? How'm I going to hold my pants up?"

"We don't want nobody hanging hisself. The paperwork's a killer when they do," the guard said. "Our tailor, he's fresh in from London, from duding up those fags they have over there. He'll be sure you have a perfect fit."

The prison processing officer scribbled on a clipboard and said, "He goes to the north wing, cellblock C. The guards will assign him a luxury suite."

"Which is the north wing?"

"The one to your left when you come in the gate."

"Wait a minute. I saw through the fence. Out in that yard, they're all rough-looking trade with tattoos. Darkies too."

"You got a problem with coloreds?"

"Not at all," Boomer said. "I hire them as lot boys. You can ask anybody."

"That real white of you."

"Now, listen here," Boomer said. "I'm an upstanding member of the community. You do the right thing and put me in with harmless mugs like tax cheats and rapists."

"We'll see what we can do. Maybe let you sleep in the warden's office."

"C'mon. Those bank robbers and killers, they'll be cornholing me in the shower."

"Should of phoned ahead for reservations," said the processing officer. "See that DeSoto parked out front?"

"What about it?"

"The warden, he bought it from you. Saw one of your commercials and drove all the way to Seattle to get screwed. Mention it and he gets more pissed off than he would if there was a riot or jail break."

A Negro guard came in for him.

Looking at him and talking fast, which he knew how to do, Boomer said, "I got nothing against the coloreds. That uppity little gal down in Alabama or wherever, as far as I'm concerned, she can ride anywhere she wants on the fucking bus. Hell, she can ride on the driver's lap. It's all the same to me. You can check out my service department. Look at my sweepers and cleanup crews. They're proof positive that I hire colored boys."

The guard stoically shook his head and steered Boomer into the depths of the state pen, pushing maybe a bit harder than he had to. Boomer would fight it legally, this railroading of him, but his funds were frozen by the IRS, which was in cahoots with creditors and Agnes. That shyster Spliff, he'd been paid off the top and had already forgotten his client's name.

Boomer had all the time in the world to make a mental list of everyone he'd get even with.

Bolling, whatever he had in mind for Peggy; that came out of thin air, even to her. Speaking of Peggy, the slut, the stool pigeon, she was high up on his list. Agnes, his shriveled prune of a wife who didn't appear once in the kangaroo court or to see him off. They all had something to gain. Humpty Dumpty too, if he'd only had the common decency to die. All his many other enemies, they'd pick his dealership clean.

That private eye. Him for sure. If not for him, the whole thing would've blown over.

Yes sir, he'd keep them all in mind, seven days a week, every waking hour, for five long years.

It'd sustain him in there with these animals, give him a reason to live.

Chapter 18

Dewey Beats Truman

*H*ERBIE BARNWELL DID COME OUT of his coma. This was a day after they locked Boomer King up in the hoosegow. His bones were healing too. The doctors were puzzled and couldn't explain his recovery.

My medical theory was he was so pickled that an infection couldn't take hold.

When I visited Herbie, part of the plaster had been chipped off, like granite in a quarry. All four scrawny appendages were exposed.

He blinked at me like a newborn.

I gave him a business card.

He focused with difficulty and said, "A private eye. What're you doing here?"

"Long story. You're my assignment," I said in a Joe Friday cadence.

That vague reply which would elicit further questions from most seemed to satisfy Herbie. He bummed a smoke off me. As I've said, I wasn't a smoker, but I always carried a pack of Lucky Strikes (an unfiltered brand, of course) to loosen up nervous interviewees. I shook one out of the pack and lit it for him, despite smoking being frowned upon in hospitals because of oxygen tents. Doctors and nurses smoked too, so why not?

I asked him if he recalled why he was in the hospital.

He took a long drag and exhaled. "I don't remember hardly nothing since Dewey beat Truman.

Got me a fierce headache though. What was I drinking last night anyways?"

I looked at one of the bags that dripped into him from a tube. "Glucose."

Just then, Darla came in, took the cigarette from him, and deposited it in a hallway ashcan as if it were a dangerous insect.

"Bad bad boy," she said. "You're putting your uncanny survival skills to the test, Uncle Herbie."

He tapped plaster with a bony finger and said, "How come this body armor they got me in reminds me of the kid nursery rhyme, Humpty Dumpty?"

"If his eggshell was that solid," I said, "He wouldn't've taken such a great fall."

"Brick, may Uncle Herbie and I have a little private time?"

I waited in the hall for her.

Teary-eyed, Darla came out and said, "King, that fucking bastard, good thing he was convicted already. Uncle Herbie doesn't remember a single, solitary thing about what he'd seen or the fall."

Kersplat.

Unable to come up with a snappier response, I said, "Well, justice was done."

"Uncle Herbie is unlikely to ever fully recover, but I'll try to make his remaining days as comfortable as I can."

"I know you will, Darla."

"I can't pay you enough, Brick. I'm so grateful."

"Forget money. My mother really wants to meet you."

"She does?"

"My star client and a celebrity victim, who wouldn't?" I said, telling her only a fraction of the story about my matchmaking mother. "She's invited us over for dinner if I give her a few hours notice.

Does tonight work for you? Afterward, come to the movies with me and we're even-steven."

"If we go to the drive-in. I don't like stuffy old theatres."

She didn't have to ask me twice.

~ ~ ~

That very night, I drove us to dinner at my mother's, a small house on Alki Avenue. She was right across the street from Puget Sound.

"You've never said anything about her, Brick."

"If she likes you, which she will, she'll tell you everything you want to know and then some."

It began with the smallest of small talk with Martha Bates serving pre-dinner whiskey sours so weak that the dominant flavor was the maraschino cherry garnish. She was a tiny woman who smiled easily, though the act appeared to cause her pain.

"One of you is driving, after all," Martha said.

At dinner, Mother said, "Brickford, are you going to finish your green beans?"

I had been maneuvering them behind a shield of meatloaf and mashed potatoes. As always, her meatloaf and potatoes were wonderful, eliciting sincere raves from Darla, but the beans came from a can and boiled within an inch of their lives.

I smiled at Darla and said, "That isn't a question, it's a command."

"Brickford?"

Whichever it was, I knew it wasn't about the grayish-green beans, it was Mother cleverly segueing to the origin of my name.

"Named for someone important in our past, Darla. With your library and history background, it might ring familiar."

"Just Brickford?"

"Haynes Brickford Bates."

"Oh my God. It does," Darla said. "I can't come up with the details, but I associate it with McCarthyism."

Mother nodded approvingly. Darla was now daughter-in-law-worthy.

Mother said, "Haynes Brickford Bates was a social reform pioneer and an officer in the Abraham Lincoln Brigade, fighting Francisco Franco and his fascists in the Spanish Civil War, where he succumbed. The odds against the Brigade and their Republican allies were overwhelming, thanks largely to the supplies and direct aid by Hitler and Mussolini. Need I mention Guernica?"

"No," Darla said. "That was an outrage against humanity."

The room had gone so quiet that her single word echoed.

"Brickford's father paid for it thanks to Senator Joseph McCarthy. He was a lefty, a pinko, and that was that. McCarthy was discredited for what he was and drank himself to death a few years later but the damage had been done. A respected high school teacher of math and physics, he couldn't get a job at the school as a janitor."

My third secret, after virginity and gun-a-phobia. No, it transcended *secret*. It was a *burden*. That I might be deemed a pinko by association or in my genes, I wore its weight every single day. If I needed another reason not to apply for a teaching job, this was it.

I waited, dreading the finish, but Mother just sighed heavily and said, "Who's ready for dessert?"

We all were: gooey brownies.

~ ~ ~

In the car I spoke of my only sibling and older sister, Julia.

"She married a very nice man. Mother and I like

him very much. They're both accountants and live in Chicago, doing very well. They moved away, I think, because of the pinko taint, what it'd do to Mother, further ostracism by so-called friends and others.

"Your father?" Darla said. "You don't have to say if you don't want to?"

"A suicide. A gun to the head halfway through my junior year, a gun I didn't know was in the house. I haven't been able to look at one since."

~ ~ ~

We did go to the drive-in, otherwise known as the passion pit, and shared a six-pack, this after a frenetic afternoon of washing and waxing the agency's '54 Ford pool car, a Mainline 4-door sedan. The springs in the seats of my '49 Merc were in worse shape than my boarding house bunk's. I attempted to clean the upholstery and hung an air freshener from the rear-view mirror. Who knows what sins had visited the interior of that car?

They were having some fun, running a double feature, *The Amazing Colossal Man* and *The Incredible Shrinking Man.*

Silly as the movies were, with the lead actor growing in one and shrinking in the other, both caused by atomic radiation, we kind of liked them until one thing led to another and we fogged the windshield. Aided by beer, I valiantly tried to unhook her bra. Inexperienced me, it was like breaking into Fort Knox, so she had to do it, with a casual behind-the-back flick. We adjourned to the back seat, laughing as we clumsily ascended and descended.

"The panty girdle is the most evil invention since the torture rack," I said, my virginal tongue loosened by the suds. "They're impossible to get off."

"No, they aren't," Darla said, removing hers, panties and all.

She whispered dirty in my ear, telling me what should occur next.

It did. A scant 30 seconds later. She concealed her disappointment. The second time, however, was as satisfying for her as for me.

To our mutual surprise, Brick Bates Junior was conceived.

Whoever said patience is a virtue has never held a
stick of
dynamite with a lighted fuse
while tracer rounds are flying over your head.
                                                    - Linus Aalborg

Chapter 19

RIP

*H*AVE YOU EVER BEEN TOLD that you'd be late for your own funeral?

It hasn't happened to me. At least not yet.

But I was late for Granduncle Herbie Barnwell's.

Sidestepping headstones and sloshing along Eternal Rest Cemetery's overwatered grounds on this warm afternoon, I spotted the awning. My grandmother, Darla Hogan Bates, and other mourners were underneath it, gathered at the rectangular hole into which Herbert Allen Barnwell, age 103, victim of a brutal homicide, had been placed.

Ironically, he had toppled off a third-floor balcony to his death, a near-identical height to the infamous 1957 brick wall at the long-defunct Boomer King DeSoto-Plymouth. Herbie hadn't been inside a plastic eggshell last week, falling on cue.

He had fallen involuntarily this last time, thanks to a blow from a blunt object that cracked the back of his skull, an object that had been left on the balcony — the presumptive murder weapon — in order to taunt the police.

An object identical to the one that had placed my grandfather, Brickford Bates the First, into a coma. A murderer who sought to be a celebrated double murderer. A sick individual taunting family, friends and law enforcement personnel.

In Granduncle Herbie's hands at the time of his nocturnal murder was a pair of binoculars. Something in his long-ago Humpty Dumpty persona had triggered Herbert Allen Barnwell's lechery, when heretofore his primary weakness was alcoholism. Herbie had been a libertine and a voyeur until his last breath, may he rest in peace, a smile on his wrinkled face.

I counted the full house. Easily 200 more people fanned out onto the lawn. Many were older women, aided by canes and walkers, in flowered dresses a generation old. Herbie's paramours? His groupies?

I didn't see Dad, but, then, I didn't expect to.

I slipped in and sat between Gramma Darla and Abigail Larsen in the seat they'd saved for me. There were so many flowers, it smelled like a florist shop. Reading from a Bible was a young reverend in a Richard Milhous Nixon ensemble of blue suit, white shirt, and dark tie. The clergyman was plump, with the blush of one freshly shaven.

Through moist eyes, Abigail (don't call me Abby!), a doppelgänger for the photos I've seen of the 1957 Darla Hogan, gave me a where-the-hell-have-you-been look. Then she squeezed my hand. I was already forgiven. Her snits went *poof* quickly, another reason why I loved her.

I couldn't truthfully blame my workload either, but in a sense I could. One of my two current clients was Mrs. Leo (Erlene) Spotts. Mrs. Spotts had hired me to dig up dirt on her separated spouse, who was sowing what passed for wild oats.

I'd been reporting to her that there was nothing to report. Her Leo *wanted* to cheat on her in the worst way, but try as he might, he was unable to score. He was not young and had a bowling-ball gut. I'd trailed Leo Spotts to all the usual singles venues — bars,

libraries, Laundromats, park benches, city buses —
and watched him drive a stake through his own heart
with clever approaches such as, "Do you come here
often?" and "Seen any neat movies lately?" and "Sure
feels like it's gonna rain." and the deadliest of them
all: "What's your sign?"

His chances of getting lucky were slim. Or getting
unlucky, I thought. None of the women he targeted
qualified as queen of the hop. The majority had fewer
teeth than Leo did and more tattoos.

I was ashamed to bill Mrs. Spotts, although I did
anyway, as the agency's cash flow was a bare trickle.
So when she called earlier today and asked if I'd
rescue her treed cat, I could not refuse. It was an
overweight orange tabby named Sweetie Pie that
would not quit meowing nor respond to our "Kitty,
kitty, nice kitty."

In a hurry and without a game plan or gloves and
proper shoes, I slowly and awkwardly crawled up a
towering weeping willow with a curved trunk. Just
between you and me, I am a master of no trade and a
jack of a few, but none required this level of dexterity.

The fire department rescued us both, so if I
blamed anybody for my tardiness to the funeral, it was
them. It took a fire truck 45 minutes to arrive;
Obviously, Mrs. Spotts's urgent call was not urgent to
them. I could only hope that the TV news team on the
scene, laughing and photographing as I was helped
down a ladder, will bump Sweetie Pie and I for a real
story. Like a caterpillar infestation or a sinkhole.

So there you are, a damned good excuse. I was on
business, on assignment. Providing I was crazy
enough to tell anyone my pathetic tale. A recent
college graduate, by default I had recently assumed
leadership of the Aalborg Detective Agency and, with
no experience whatsoever, was trying to prove myself

to the veteran staff (of two) by taking cases that wouldn't jeopardize relationships with longstanding clients (very very few).

The minister began what I hoped was a closing prayer, the 23rd Psalm. That's the one that often wraps these things up. No such luck. After the" amen", he turned a page and continued reading something or another in King James English.

Abigail squeezed my hand harder. Off to each side, flanking the mourners were two police detectives. I recognized one; Detective Harrison, who gave me the high sign as he scanned the mourners, letting me know he was still working Gramps' case and had been assigned to the Herbert Barnwell homicide too.

Chapter 20

Brick Bates Junior

WAS I AN AGORAPHOBE WHO COULD NOT even go out the door to attend a funeral of a man whose life was so importantly interwoven with mine? A man who was peripherally responsible for the shotgun wedding of my parents?

Call it what you wish, but I was suffering from a midlife crisis that had become chronic.

I had turned over the agency to my son the moment he removed his cap and gown. Sandwiched in the family tree between two born detectives, while my one and only niche in the profession was forensic accounting. Tax fraud, bankruptcy shenanigans, and the meatiest of them all, money laundering.

But thanks to the Aalborg Detective Agency's hardboiled heritage, clients were far and few between. The curse of Linus Aalborg. You did not turn to a commando to audit the books; you went to him to throttle the bookkeeper.

Was I depressed after the attack on my father that left him comatose? Do I fear for my own safety that I'm next on a serial killer's list, number three in line?

Without a doubt, all of the above, I thought as I peeked between the front curtains of my condo.

What the hell was I on the lookout for on this fine afternoon besides a bloodthirsty maniac? Resentful mourners carrying torches?

Was it unprofessional of me to take a "leave of absence" as owner and private eye in charge of the Aalborg Detective Agency, dumping it on the sole remaining agent to hold down the fort until my son and only child finished his last quarter of college? Handing him the keys to the agency when he was as green as a gherkin and still is?

Chickenshit was the operative word.

So be it. The Humpty Dumpty madness was rearing its head again and I could not cope.

I was thinking this for the thousandth time as I retreated to the sanctuary of my darkened living room. I channel surfed, just me, myself and 871 channels on a 70-inch curved-screen HDTV.

Newton Minow, Chairman of the FCC in the Kennedy Administration, famously called television a "vast wasteland". The quote was made 50-plus years ago, an era of vacuum tubes and black-and-white screens.

The high-minded contended that nothing had changed. If anything, programming had gotten much worse. I had no problem with that evaluation. Ninety percent of what's on today was garbage, but it was my garbage to consume with my eyes and ears.

I paused at a cooking show, the hottest genre on the tube these days. It was a competition among chefs from restaurants I would never visit, concocting dishes I would never eat.

Whoever whipped up the worst dish utilizing haggis, razor clams, kale, and duck fat was eliminated on this round.

I was spellbound.

Chapter 21

Detective Juan Diego Harrison

"YOU'RE NOT AFRICAN AMERICAN," I had said when Detective Harrison came to my dorm room several months ago. I was cramming for finals and was a little punchy. A black Detective Harrison prominent in my life long before my birth had shoehorned itself into my thoughts and common sense.

The names were coincidences. My Detective Harrison's face was the hue of a Native American and his aquiline profile jibed with limestone carvings I'd seen of the ancient Maya.

"No shit," Detective Harrison said as he put away his ID. "My old man was a religious nut who didn't spare the rod. He was a Christian missionary who went on down to the Yucatán Peninsula to make a nuisance of himself. He was using the ol' bullshit missionary come-on that they were doing 'language studies'.

"He met my mom in a village. She wasn't interested in being converted to the Jesus fan club, but she converted him into a human being, more or less. The conversion didn't take for long. He knocked her up, they got married, came home, and he promptly ran off with a church secretary. She had big hair, tits and a room-temperature IQ. Just his speed.

"My first and middle names are Juan and Diego. Know who Juan Diego was?"

"I'm minoring in history. The name rings a bell."

"Ringing the bell won't win you an A. Juan Diego

was a little Mexican boy who in 1531 conveniently saw the Virgin Mary."

"Oh yeah. The Virgin of Guadalupe," I said.

"There you go. The sighting greased the skids for the Spaniards to flog the love of Jesus into the savages. The little guy was even made a saint. It was my old man's idea to name me that. My mom thought it was stupid, but he won out."

"Is your mother living with you?"

"She was before she died of cancer two years ago."

"Sorry."

"So are we, my wife and three kids and I."

"I guess you're not here to conduct a history seminar."

Detective Harrison wasn't. His voice softening, he went on to tell me that my grandfather had been attacked and left for dead, and what was known about it so far, which was basically nothing.

My elderly grandfather, the first Brick Bates, had been found by a neighbor inside the front door of his condo, his and Gramma Darla's. She was at work at the family's detective agency and the front door was ajar. The back of his skull was broken and the weapon, a hood ornament from a car dating to the 1950's, was beside him.

He said, "Either he left it there carelessly or for us to find. This asshole has some kind of warped moxie."

Gramps Brick was taken to a hospital, Detective Harrison went on. He was in a coma and not expected to survive.

"Excuse me."

I rushed down the hall into the can, locked myself in a stall, and cried and puked. Gramps Bates, retired after years of heading the agency, dodging literal and figurative bullets, beginning with Boomer King's threat when he was being hauled away to jail in 1957, and, six decades later, some fucking coward smacked him in the back of the head.

Gramps Brick Bates the First, age 82, was the nicest person you'd ever want to meet.

Life ain't fair. That's one helluva lot more than a cliché.

Composure regained, I went back to my room.

"How's my grandmother doing?"

"As well as can be expected. Friends and neighbors are with her. She's one tough lady."

"An ornament from what kind of car?" I said.

"We're researching," he said, showing me a picture. "No prints, of course. It's chrome-plated pot metal, not cheap plastic like they all are these days. That sucker's a two-handled hatchet."

Two-handled hatchet was an apt description. Centered by the DeSoto crest, the ornament was easily 18 inches long. It had horizontal arms and weighed two or three pounds.

"It's from a 1957 DeSoto Adventurer," I said.

He looked at me. "You're sure?"

"I am. I've studied the Humpty Dumpty case thoroughly," I said, summarizing it from Herbie Barnwell's hard fall off the wall to the subsequent arrest of Horace (Boomer) King, much of it due to the dogged investigative work done by my grandparents.

I then asked if he was related to that Detective Harrison, the officer who over half a century ago snapped the cuffs on Boomer King.

"To the best of my knowledge, I'm not related to the man. I have no relative, past or present, in police work," he said. "Harrison's not as common as Smith or Jones, but there are ample numbers of us. What ever became of all those nice folks besides your grandmother?"

"Well, believe it or not, Herbie Barnwell is still

alive, and over one hundred. He's in an old folks home after being kicked out of another one at age ninety-two for drunkenness and sexual harassment of female residents. He had thirteen stitches from knitting needle wounds after he slipped his hand under a lady's dress while she was making a shawl. A big mistake on his part.

"They showed him the door after he recovered. It wasn't his first infraction. He's settled down. That or he's getting away with things. Herbie was a Peeping Tom too. His binoculars were confiscated I don't know how many times. Juiced to the gills at my fifteenth birthday party, he told me it was his favorite sport, but what he saw on the Humpty Dumpty wall was the all-time highlight."

Detective Harrison grinned and nodded approvingly. "I envy the man's genes. The other players in your Humpty Dumpty studies?"

"Boomer King was released from the state prison in 1962, a year or so after Chrysler stopped making DeSotos. He'd had a rough time of it in the pen from other inmates. They say he survived due to him assembling a neo-Nazi skinhead type group out of the worst, toughest, hard-case white prisoners."

"They did that back then?"

"King was a pioneer at that too, along with his bizarre TV commercials, if pioneer's the right word for the man. I haven't the foggiest where that sick brainstorm came from. He was no kid when he was sent up, over fifty. He got out alive, but his health was broken. He died several years later, a penniless drunk."

"The woman, Peggy."

"Peggy's whole name at that time was Margaret Hardin Callahan King Bolling. She was a blonde bombshell for sure. Who knows if she's still alive? She divorced her husband at the time of the affair with Boomer. Eddie Callahan, a tool-and-die maker, was the lucky ex-husband, a man with plenty of behavioral problems of his own. She then married Boomer King while he was in prison, shortly prior to his release. It didn't work out.

"Soon thereafter, Ken Bolling and Peggy became man and wife too, albeit briefly. Bolling had brought her a fresh rose every day during the trial proceedings that sent Boomer to the pen, you know, so he'd been pining for her for who knows how long."

"A fun lady," Harrison said.

"During a drunken and protracted weekend, Peggy and Kenneth flew to Tijuana or Reno — I don't recall which — where she obtained a divorce from Boomer King and married Bolling. The marriage lasted a month longer than the drunken weekend. Somehow, Kenneth Bolling acquired an interest in the dealership after the IRS and creditors had picked it clean. It quickly disintegrated and became an equally doomed Studebaker franchise, then a used car lot for junkers. Bolling married and divorced twice or three times more. There were children too."

"You've done your homework," Juan Diego Harrison said.

Detective work, I wanted to say. "Thanks. It's been kind of an obsession."

He closed his notebook and stood. "What are your plans after college?"

"I graduate in June. After some partying and vacation, I'll go to work for the agency. Taking it over actually."

"A big agency? I'm not familiar with it."

"No. Grandma Darla is on the front desk, really the person in charge. There's only one agent now besides my father, an older guy. The agency is hanging on by its fingernails."

"You're not majoring in police science?"

"No. Like I said, history, with an English minor," I said, not specifying that my major was art history, which probably didn't qualify in his mind as real history to the average person.

"What's the name of your agency again?"

"The Aalborg Detective Agency, named after its founder, Linus Aalborg, who escaped the Nazis and fought in the Norwegian underground. He was part of the team that blew up their heavy water plant, which was instrumental in the development of an atomic bomb. Ike and Churchill pinned medals on him."

"Too bad the killer didn't come after him with a hood ornament. He'd have his hands full. Contact me if anything new comes up."

~ ~ ~

At the here and now, at the cemetery service we met Detective Harrison outside after most everyone had paid their respects to Herbie Barnwell and dispersed.

"Any insights?" I said.

"Couldn't tell you if there were. How many of these 1957 DeSotos are there in the world?" he asked.

"Two too many," Abigail said.

"Our budget's a joke," Harrison said to Gramma Darla. "But I can try to arrange protection for you, ma'am."

"The shithead who's doing this will need protection if I get to the motherfucker first," Gramma Darla said.

If anybody doubted her, they weren't saying. Certainly not Detective Harrison, whose mouth was hanging open.

Chapter 22

Brick Bates I

DO NOT ASK ME HOW I KNOW, but I know you're there and I know who you are. I know infinitely more than you or the doctors think I know. All the doctors know is what they see and read on the laptops and gauges and green screens, the monotonous sine curves. Curves which I'll take over a horizontal flatline, thank you very much.

I know when I have visitors. I know not by sight, sound, touch or smell, but by their essence, whatever the hell that means. When I come out of this, I'll try to explain what "essence" means if I can remember experiencing anyone's essence. And the essence of this otherworldly experience.

I know when a visitor "packs heat". They were by early on, one in particular, probably the detective in charge of my case. I even know what he carried: a nine-millimeter automatic that holds 19 rounds. The brand name escapes me.

I know that the "heat" spikes the lines and numbers on the readouts. I know they don't know why. Doctors look and call in more doctors, and nobody has a clue. They never will, as my irrational fear of firearms is and will forever be my deepest, darkest secret.

What none of us know is when it'll be over. I know, I know, it ain't over till it's over. Unless they decide I'm a hopeless vegetable and pull the plugs.

If I check out, I have a hunch that it'll be like a chain being pulled on a light fixture: total darkness.

Which will be a good trick since I already inhabit darkness 24/7.

Maybe I'll be reassigned to a black hole type of darkness, the mother of all Darknesses, a theoretical celestial object with a gravitational tug so ferocious that it sucks in everything within a million light years, including light.

Believe me, I am in no hurry to satisfy my curiosity.

If I snap out of this a la the 1957-model Herbie Barnwell, I will not remember what I know and you do not know. Other than Truman beat Dewey in 1948. This is okay with me.

Whoever did this took me from behind.

A hard blow to the back of my skull.

Then Ken Bolling's *kersplat* a la Herbie/Humpty

Darla is here now. She is here often, as often as she can. Her hand is on my atrophied arm.

Darla Hogan Bates gently wipes away the tear. I wish she wouldn't. The tear is a part of her.

I smell her shampoo and perfume. It is the exact same aroma I smelled on that hyper-magical night at which growing and shrinking movie characters flickered while Darla and I were in the back seat of the agency pool car, the 1954 Ford Mainline 4-door sedan.

Preparing to leave, she kisses my forehead, upon which falls another tear.

I've been fantasizing her as the Princess and me the Frog Prince. No such luck yet. I remain on the lily pad, awaiting magic.

Chapter 23

An Honest Woman/Man

GRAMMA DARLA PLAYS CUPID with the subtlety of a bullhorn and a white shotgun. She keeps telling me to make an honest woman of Abigail, and keeps nudging Abigail to make a proper swain out of me, an honest man, as it were.

Abigail won't hear of it. She is some years older than me and has a high-paying software job. I don't understand her title, let alone what she does: She's a Senior Software Developer in Charge of Core Communication Cloud Technology. That's clear enough, kind of, cloud or no cloud. But what she uses to develop the software that develops the other stuff—C/C++ and .NET and TCP and UDP and VoIP and SQL and Agile and XP and Bibbidi Bobbidi Boo. We're talking 21st-Century Ancient Greek here.

She's the brains of the outfit (her and me), so if she ever decides we should consider making her An Honest Woman, then we'll explore the matter further.

Abigail and I did have a "unhoneymoon" after my college graduation, which Gramma Darla believed was scandalous, but who was she to talk in that regard? We went to Ecuador, to Cuenca, Guayaquil, the Galapagos Islands, and Quito. The trip was fun and culture rolled into one, and in our mind legitimized our moving in together.

"Living in sin," Gramma Darla termed it. "Shacked up like two dogs in heat out on a curb in front of God and everyone."

It was all I could do to remind her that my father,

who was born six-and-a-half months before she married my Gramps was *not* premature. Not at eight pounds, three ounces. That'd make the Guinness Book of World Records for preemies.

Abigail Larsen and I met two years ago when I worked at the agency as a summer intern. I was assigned her case because it promised to be time-consuming, promised little continuing revenue, and got me out of everybody's hair.

She was being stalked by her ex-husband. They had married just out of high school, a blunder as so many of those youthful marriages are. She soon recognized it, but he didn't.

He followed her around like a demented puppy and called her at all hours, no matter how many times she changed her unlisted number.

Abigail wanted me to track the sicko and to dig up dirt that would discourage him from stalking her and hopefully land him in the pokey too. But he was as clean as the clichéd whistle. He lived with his mother, taught Sunday school, and was secretary-treasurer of the local orchid society.

Even then, I knew the type. One fine day, he'd go berserk. Then he'd be a model prisoner on death row.

I'd flipped for Abigail big time. My feelings for her grew daily. Exponentially. I took her and her case deep inside my heart. I stalked the freakoid as he stalked her. One night when he was parked across from her condo, I decided I'd had a bellyful.

I sneaked up on him and took the law into my own hands, as well as various body parts I used as handles with which to deautomobile the rancid son of a bitch.

I'm no 97-pound weakling, nor am I the celluloid PI who effortlessly kicks ass. I was in the midrange, and accomplished this mission thanks to passion and adrenaline.

I never told Abigail what I did to him and I'm not telling anybody else, other than that he moved in with a maiden aunt on the opposite coast and is eligible to try out for the Vienna Boys Choir.

She rewarded me by returning my affection. And it wasn't just heroism. She collected old vinyl and said I bore a close resemblance to a singer from the fifties named Buddy Holly, including my choice of eyeglasses. And, concomitantly, devirginating yours truly after a candlelit dinner in her condo.

I was about to apply a Bunsen burner to the pudding to caramelize it (recipe I found online and memorized earlier that day) when we spontaneously chose to have each other for dessert, her taking the lead, discarding articles of clothing on the floor from the dinette to her bed.

~ ~ ~

At dinner this evening, I recapped events of the case. And a Vital Mystery Clue she unearthed late this afternoon from an Internet cubbyhole only computer experts like her could reach into. Us at the Aalborg Agency might as well have been using Commodore 64s.

"Margaret (Peggy) Jones Hardin Callahan King Bolling Miller Parker Jacobs Smith lives here in the county in a senior's apartment," she said. "If Detective Harrison hasn't pinned her down yet, it's due to all the surnames tacked on since she was Ms. Bolling. Her last, Smith, is so common. Also, she'd moved around a lot when she was younger."

Abigail was a vegetarian on the verge of evangelizing me. Tonight we were having her incredibly hearty and easy-to-make Meatlessloaf, a recipe she did not mind sharing with one and all.

Time of preparation, including baking and cleanup: 1-½ hours.

Ingredients:

1. Two packages of 90-second whole grain rice — your choice of plain or flavored.

2. One bag of spinach, kale, or field greens — your choice.

3. Chop the greens finely.

4. Nuke the rice packets.

5. Mix the rice and greens in a large bowl.

6. Mix in the desired amount of jarred pesto.

7. Mix in the desired amount and type of shredded cheese.

8. Pour the mixture into a glass loaf pan that has been coated with cooking-oil spray.

9. Bake at 350° for 45 minutes.

10. Optimally, it should cure overnight in the fridge to fully blend the flavors and set up.

It pairs nicely with a California zinfandel and serves 3 to 4.

Abigail claims to have made over 500 Meatlessloaves over the years, each one a bit different; she likens them to snowflakes. Instead of pesto, perhaps use salsa, Italian sauce, or vindaloo. Also, add oatmeal, caramelized onions, hot sauce, shredded carrots, *ad infinitum*.

A Meatlessloaf, she said, if it needs a further recommendation, is an excellent instrument for cleaning out the fridge.

Atop all her skills and responsibilities, Abigail Larsen served as president of the condominium owners' association. Woe be it to any owner who arbitrarily decided to stop paying dues or cause trouble. She ruled the 130-unit COA with velvet gloves that concealed brass knuckles.

"Should we pass this along to Detective Harrison?" I said.

"What do you think?"

"Eventually," I said. "She's not going anywhere, is she?"

"No. No she isn't." Abigail said, "I wonder what ever happened to Ken Bolling?"

"We know nothing after the whirlwind romance with Peggy and a couple of failed marriages later. He'd be well into his eighties if he's still alive."

She said, "Too old to be hatcheting people with a hood ornament."

Abigail said, "I'm working at home this week. Tomorrow, why don't you and I pay a call on Ms. Peggy?"

I said, "I think she'd love the company."

Chapter 24

Margaret (Peggy) Jones Hardin Callahan King Bolling Miller Parker Jacobs Smith

PEGGY LIVED IN A LOW-INCOME SENIORS' COMPLEX south of town in the south burbs, in a DMZ between Kent and Auburn. Three stories and pale green, it had a depressing, institutional look. There were a number of full-sized 1990s sedans in the parking lot, presumably many of them one-owner, low-milers. I thought of Boomer King for no particular reason, in no particular context. I suppose because these odometers hadn't been rolled back.

When we arrived, she was being served, ironically and semi-coincidentally, a meatloaf lunch.

Abigail stood by Peggy's opened door as I went to her mini-dinette and asked if I could have a few moments of her time.

With a loose-denture grin, she looked around the meals-for-seniors server and said to me, "Take me out for a decent meal and I'll think about it. Make it a big steak with all the trimmings and you can count on getting lucky when we come back here. Or in the car if you and your hormones can't wait."

"Now now, Mrs. Smith," said her server.

"Are you married, kiddo?"

I replied by withdrawing my notebook.

If I concentrated, I could see the resemblance between her and the 1957 Peggy in the file photos. But there was considerably more of today's Peggy and gravity was claiming it. Her hair was as platinum as it was six decades earlier, albeit substantially thinner.

She wore heavy blue eye shadow and ruby red lipstick. She looked like the handiwork of a mortuary cosmetologist.

I said, "Sorry to barge in, Mrs. Smith, but I'm sorry to report that Herbie Barnwell is deceased."

She paused, then said, "Well, that's the way the cookie crumbles. You're a young pup, but a dead ringer for the private eye who along with that fucking drunk Herbie ruined our lives, me and Horace's."

The server shook her head and said, "Your language, Mrs. Smith."

"Don't let the door hit you in the ass, Dorothy," Peggy told her.

When we had the tiny apartment to ourselves, I said, "He was seriously injured when he played Humpty Dumpty, you know. Boomer King went to prison for attempted murder."

She snapped bony fingers. "Horace tried to give you a deal on a car for keeping your trap shut and you turned it down, didn't he? You dummy. A brand-new DeSoto Adventurer. That car's a classic today."

"That was my grandfather, not me, Peggy," I said, resisting the urge to begin a hopeless debate that it wasn't a deal, but rather a *bribe*.

"Are you aware that my grandfather was recently put in a coma after being hit in the head by a 1957 DeSoto Adventurer hood ornament?"

Peggy cackled and looked upward. "Horace, are you pulling some magic from up there?"

I said nothing.

She looked at the floor. "Or from down there? That's more your speed, you pussy-hound, cheating rascal, you. Not that you were any worse than my other ex-louses. I sure can pick 'em, can't I? Horace?"

I didn't reply.

Peggy squinted at me. "Why're you here? What

skin is this off your nose?"

"It appears that a potential killer is on the loose. You have the right to be warned and the obligation to provide any pertinent information."

"If I know anything and I don't, I tell nobody. Hell, I don't know for sure who you are."

I put a business card on her small dining table. She squinted at it and said, "The one husband I ever had who wasn't a bum all the time, only half the time, was Horace, and you went and sent him off to prison and killed him. You can go straight to hell!"

Chapter 25

The Albanian Highway System

I DROPPED ABIGAIL OFF AT HOME so she could get back to work doing what she does, then went in to the office. Abigail felt as I did, that Peggy lived it such a time warp that it'd be nigh impossible to sift a Vital Mystery Clue from her delusions even if she possessed an investigative gem.

Our current office was across the street from the original Aalborg Agency, which may or may not have been established in 1928 or 1938 or 1945 (if one swallowed our boilerplate tale of the heroic Linus Aalborg, which I kind of did and maybe still do, as it's romantic as all hell). Early troubles with the police, the FBI, clients, revenuers, the IRS and lawyers made the agency's true genealogy obscure.

I must admit, while I continue to enjoy the Linus Aalborg quotations, I've never studied the photographs of Mr. Aalborg in detail, in particular the ones where he was awarded medals by the World War Two luminaries. I didn't want to be disillusioned.

That building had been torn down years ago in an urban renewal project. In its place was a multi-level concrete parking garage, a dubious improvement. The iconic Smith Tower was no longer visible, surrounded in a forest of high-rises.

We're on the third floor now, with an elevator, no less. Fellow tenants include bail bondsmen, lawyers who come and go with an aura of ambulance fumes, and those whose doors and spots on the directory are unnamed.

There were some changes inside the Aalborg too, most notably computers, laptop lids upraised at desks no longer occupied by detectives. It was an illusion of prosperity and of agents in the field. The office had the artificiality of a TV newsroom.

When we did have business, it was most often conducted the old-fashioned way, on telephones and by burning shoe leather. Clients schooled by TV private eyes liked what they saw.

It was a shirtsleeve environment, every day a casual day. But if you smoked, you did so out in the alley, an unpopular rule by many in our building, instituted by my father, now backed up by the state legislature. Unlike fictional private eyes, there was not a single gun on a person or in inventory.

For this I was thankful; my deepest secret was a pathological fear of firearms. Where that phobia came from, I haven't an inkling. It had been with me since my earliest memory for reasons unknown, and there was no indication that it'd ever go away.

Photos of two ex-Aalborg owners hung on the walls. A couple of hard-looking characters named Buck and Spike, posing with cigarettes in the mouths and automatic pistols in their shoulder holsters. They ran Aalborg over half a century ago, legendary for the direct approach they took in solving cases for their clients. They were no strangers to self-induced trouble either.

Gramma Darla was already back at the reception desk, where she's worked since retiring from the library system fourteen years ago. She was 83-years-old, tyrannical, earthy and adorable. She was said to share traits with the also-legendary Marge who ruled the front desk for eons. Marge passed away not long ago at the age of 92, in a trailer park at which she had resided with her eighth or ninth husband, a retired Fuller Brush Man.

We'd all encouraged Gramma Darla to take some time off, traumatized as she was by the attack on Gramps. She adamantly refused, arguing that staying busy was the "best medicine".

Without her, it would be just the other agent and I. Unspoken was the fact that the Aalborg Agency was also on financial life support.

The large powerhouse agencies with all their technology could do what we could do in a week in five minutes, and the industry itself was dying slowly compressing. Thanks to the Internet, the average person could play Sherlock Holmes.

I proved it myself by Googling the first silly thing that popped into my head: Highways in Albania.

In five seconds, there it was, seven pages worth. Did I know that the total length of Albania's roads doubled in the three decade after World War Two? Or that SH2, between the capital of Tirana and Durres was the first highway to be constructed after communism?

Now I did.

"Hi, Gramma."

"Goddammit, don't call me Gramma in here. How many times do I have to remind you? I'm Ms. Bates. Talk to me."

Gramma had a salty mouth, but at least it was a normal part of her speech and not spoken with Ms. Margaret (Peggy) Smith's bitter malice.

I filled her in on my visit to Peggy.

"We'd better keep an eye on her," Ms. Bates said. "Just because her hot pants haven't shrunk and withered away doesn't mean she doesn't know more than she's letting on."

She gave me a telephone message, saying, "What do you make of this?"

It was from Dad. He wanted to see me ASAP.

"He'd called before we opened and left it on voice mail so he didn't have to speak to an actual person. Par for the course."

"I'm off to see Dad now."

"I do worry about that boy of mine."

"Me too."

"Talk sense into him. I'm hoarse from trying."

"It'll be futile."

"Try anyway. All that TV rots your brain from the inside out." She sighed heavily. "Daytime is the worst, the talk shows that tell you how to live your life. The stupid guests on them. You'll get brain cancer."

"I'll really try, Ms. Bates."

First I went to my desk to check email. Nothing going on. It was another sleepy day at the Aalborg Agency.

Fred Hudson, our lone investigator, was in his cubicle. He'd been with the agency longer than my father. He'd signed on soon after Buck was arrested and Spike had his second drug-induced heart attack and retired. Fred was a nephew or something of Buck; this was never made clear and I was so grateful that he was staying aboard this sinking ship after I took the helm.

A large man of indeterminate age with a crew cut and a vaguely Bohemian quality, Fred was an insurance specialist.

If a company believed a personal injury claim was fraudulent they came to us, specifically Fred. He was relentless and cunning. Every Whiplash Willie-type lawyer in town had screaming nightmares about Fred Hudson.

I told him about the day's activities, less my misadventure with Mrs. Spotts.

"How is your grandmother holding up after the latest?" he said softly.

"On the surface, fine."

"I have noticed no change in her demeanor."

"You won't."

"I have known Darla for ages, Brick. Solution of the crimes and vengeance keep her going."

It dawned on me for the first time that Fred Hudson did not speak in contractions.

"Not the worst of motivations."

A day without a dead Nazi's blood on my bayonet is a day without sunshine.

- Linus Aalborg

Chapter 26

Brick Bates II & III

AT DAD'S PLACE, I USUALLY had to knock and knock and knock, and ID myself two or three times, once even slipping my driver's license under the door, but he flung the door open after the first tap.

"Get in here, dammit!"

Puzzled, I did and trailed him into the living room, head down, a habit from childhood when I knew I was in for it.

He pointed at the TV and played with his well-worn remote control. Numbers, symbols, and words were worn off half the keys.

"Look!"

There I was on the 70-inch curved-screen HDTV, in Mrs. Leo Spotts's weeping willow tree with Sweetie Pie. The cat looked a helluva lot calmer than I did. They did a close-up of my white-knuckled grip on the limb as Sweetie Pie yawned.

In shock, I said, "Isn't this too early for the local evening news?"

"This is a 24-hour cable news station."

"Oops."

"Seen by who knows how many millions of viewers."

As my cell phone rang the theme music of the original Jack Webb *Dragnet,* I watched the fire department ladder lean to the rescue, firemen smirking, bringing Sweetie Pie down first.

"Mr. Bates, this is Erlene Spotts."

"Well, hi."

"I don't know if you've been watching the news."

"I'm afraid so."

"Well, so has Leo. He's insanely jealous of you, Mr. Bates."

"He is?"

"So jealous that he came home to me." She giggled. "I won't tell you what that dirty old man and I have been doing this afternoon."

Please don't, I thought, unable to speak.

"Send me your final bill," she said, her giggles interrupted by hoarse sighs. "I'll no longer require your services."

I said I would and hung up, all the while under my father's withering glare.

Before he could get after me again, I told him about Granduncle Herbie's funeral, all the mourners and curious it drew, about Gramps unchanged condition, in case he hadn't heard.

He hadn't. He had bolted himself in against reality.

Long before he handed me the keys to the agency and ran out the door, my mother, his wife, may have seen this coming. Seven years ago, she ran off with a stockbroker. They subsequently dropped out of mainstream society, and were in Vermont, living in the woods, making maple syrup. It was difficult to recognize her voice on the phone, she sounded so happy.

The TV, my old man's day and night companion, was gospel. If it wasn't on the tube, he didn't know it. He hadn't returned a voice mail or email in weeks.

"Yes. Please, Dad, snap out of it. You need us and we need you."

My plea didn't work. He started channel-surfing, his retreat into his bat cave and my exit cue.

Chapter 27

The Thinker

I RETURNED TO THE OFFICE. Gramma Darla/Ms. Bates was by herself.

"Well?" she said.

I shrugged.

She sighed. "There were times I should have taken that boy over my knee, but didn't. I spared the rod and messed up the child."

Same could be said for my maple-syrup making mother.

I sat down at my desk and couldn't help but notice that the desktop background on my computer was Sweetie Pie and I in the weeping willow. Good news travels fast. Somebody on the janitorial staff had some fun. I'd have to check with building security and tell them to provide us some.

Another objective is the completion of the Tirana-Elbasan Highway Motorway including the Krabe Tunnel,

I replaced my desktop with the prior, a photo in our sales brochure of our founder, Linus Aalborg, the great man's muscular arms folded, wearing a bandolier clustered with bullets and grenades. He was standing by a cliff, en route to destroy the Nazi's heavy water facility in Norway.

Mrs. Spotts was my one active case and the office, thanks to Gramma Darla, pretty much ran itself. I made Gramps' assault and Herbert Barnwell's murder my *ultra* priority. Of course, this was police business, not mine, but this was far more important than any

Aalborg Agency case that might come through our door, certainly treed cats.

I got online, printed out some material, and drove to the address of the former Boomer King DeSoto-Plymouth agency. No huge surprise; it had been demolished, Humpty Dumpty wall and all. In its place was a cheesy-looking mattress store, an enterprise Granduncle Herbie might have appreciated. Sale prices for a great choice of soft landing materials were plastered in the windows, used-car-lot-esque.

We were virtually in the shadow of a freeway interchange at I-5 and I-90. Seattle's very own spaghetti junction. The neighborhood had no choice but to be desolate and grubby.

Detective Harrison was in the mattress store lot, sitting on a fender of his Crown Vic squad car, fist to his chin.

"The Thinker."

"What?"

"The bronze statue by Auguste Rodin."

"Right. Of course. You majored in egghead, didn't you?"

"That's one way of putting it."

"You're wondering what I'm doing here?"

"Well, yeah."

"I'm on break, waiting for a hunch to pop into my head."

A Vital Mystery Clue, a stilted term that was been passed down the agency over the years. "Has it?"

"Nope, but I ran down the Peggy gal."

"That's great. What did you learn?" I said innocently.

"That she was mighty curious about my marital status and wasn't prejudiced against, and I quote, colored boys and the high-yellow."

"Sounds like the Peggy I remember from stories."

"Yeah. She made my day."

"Any conclusions?"

"Yeah," Harrison said. "Our perp's a nutcase who's probably been banging his own head with those hood ornaments."

I handed Detective Harrison the printouts.

"Doing my work for me? Didn't I just say, this is my lucky day?" He read them and narrated, "The city tax man's history of this property. After Boomer King went away, the place soon fell apart. It became a Studebaker agency. We know what became of them. It was a half-dozen used car lots over the years.

"Ten years ago, someone made a theme restaurant out of it, The DeSoto Sports Bar and Grill. Must've cost a fortune to plumb and rewire. It soon went belly-up and sat vacant till the mattress store."

I said, "What jumped off the page at me was the name of the first used car dealer. Ken Bolling. He was Boomer King's sales manager."

"So?"

"Peggy's fourth husband was Ken Bolling too. I don't know if it's the same Ken Bolling or a relation or not who ran the used car lot."

Detective Harrison nodded and said, "I don't believe in coincidences either."

Chapter 28
Our Archivist

ACK AT THE OFFICE, Fred Hudson was on the phone, shaking his head and smiling as he spoke. I smiled too, picturing a lawyer on the other end, sweating bullets.

"Please do not recite the law to me, sir, for I am willing to concede that your knowledge is light-years superior to mine, regardless of how many times you may have failed the bar exam before at long last becoming an attorney, and that when our client's policyholder recklessly careened into the rear of your client, doing the staggering amount of $256.84 damage to repair a catastrophic dimple on the soft-plastic rear bumper cover, and grievously injuring said client, rendering him a cripple for life, the salient point of our conversation is the video we have of him, chiropractor's back brace off, chopping a cord of wood, so I have taken the liberty of sending you a copy of the video along with a offer that is conspicuously less than your ludicrous demand on behalf of your client. Substantially less."

When he was finished, I asked his opinion on Ken Bolling's role in the murder and attempted-murder.

He said, "His marriage to Peggy lasted a month longer than the drunken weekend. She had married Horace while he was in prison. Somehow, in the interim, Kenneth Bolling acquired an interest in the dealership. It quickly disintegrated and became an equally doomed Studebaker franchise. Horace King was not pleased about that or most else. He promptly divorced her upon his release and drank himself to death, penniless."

"If Boomer King was out to get my grandfather, it'd be tough to do from beyond the grave."

"Indeed."

"Those hood ornaments. That's beyond wacky."

"I presume the police are researching recent acquisition of them," Hudson said.

"I'm sure they are, but it'd be too easy," I said. "Somebody selling them all over eBay? I doubt it."

He said, "Me too. But if somebody stockpiled them in the past and harbored a grudge. Or passed along a vendetta."

"For this many years? And where did they come from?"

"From 1957 DeSoto Adventurers," he said.

I smiled. I think he might have been having fun with me on that one, but it was impossible to tell from his poker face, a countenance that struck cold fear in the Whiplash Willies of the world. We at Aalborg thought of Fred as a mental archivist. He could write a book about the agency. From memory. Five hundred pages plus bibliography and notes.

"Fred, not everybody has a backyard full of DeSotos."

"Ah, but as early as 1957, there were rumors that Chrysler was planning to kill the DeSoto brand, which it did in late 1960, with the 1961 models the very last. The cars had been selling badly, often competing with automobiles in their own Dodge division. Buyers did not wish the burden of a mechanical orphan. Dealers who refused to let them go at a loss were stuck with them."

"Dealers like Boomer King DeSoto-Plymouth."

Fred said, "Alas, yes. Studebakers in the showroom, DeSotos in the back lot. The stench of automotive death. His Humpty Dumpty notoriety kept customers away too, thanks to excellent work by

Brick Bates the First and Ms. Darla Hogan Bates. How is he doing, by the way?"

I rocked a hand. "The same. We aren't optimistic."

"I am so sorry."

"Thanks. Those DeSotos in the lot had hood ornaments, two-handled hatchets, per Detective Harrison. They may have been stockpiled by someone willing to wait."

"In a steel and glass sense, a festering sore," Hudson said.

Gary Alexander

He was a proud Hitler Youth alum.
I cut off his singing of the Nazi's unholy anthem,
The Horst Wessel Song, in mid-chorus.
As well as his vocal cords.

- Linus Aalborg

Chapter 29

Peggy Redux

MARGARET (PEGGY) JONES HARDIN Callahan King Bolling Miller Parker Jacobs Smith must have been lonely. She was even happy to see Brick Bates again, even if he was the man largely responsible for ruining her life.

"You were such a snoop. You didn't have to hound Horace."

"That's in the job description, ma'am," I said.

"And you're the little girl he's dating?"

Abigail had asked to tag along again, partly out of sympathy for the woman, partly out of fascination, as if she were an intriguing anachronism, a living artifact. We were uncomfortable humoring Peggy in a deceptive manner, but if we could settle her into the last century and have a few questions answered, we'd be on our way. Gramma Darla was with us too, standing aside until needed.

"Yes, yes, I am," Abigail said.

"Make sure he uses protection, honey. The promises they give, they don't mean diddly shit. Lordy, they'll say *anything* to get into your drawers."

Abigail looked at me and rolled her eyes. "Don't I know."

Peggy cackled. "Cross your legs on 'em and they'll promise you the sun and the moon, won't they?"

Involuntarily, I blushed appropriately and asked, "What do you hear from Ken Bolling these days?"

"Who?"

She seemed genuinely confused, so I was

prepared to drop it and leave, but Gramma Darla walked in from the doorway. In fact, she'd practically pleaded to come along. There had been a bond in 1957 between her and Peggy I didn't quite understand, a bond of which she had refused to elaborate.

"Oh my living God," Peggy said, bursting into tears.

"There there," Gramma Darla said. "There there."

"My rock to lean on," Peggy said as they hugged.

Gramma Darla wiped her eyes as they separated and said, "Ken Bolling?"

Peggy fluttered a gnarled hand, bouncing back into her version of reality. "Oh, I hear far far too much. He won't leave me alone. The man's hornier than a three-peckered goat."

"He's been here recently?" Abigail asked.

"A day or two ago, I had to chase him out of here. Oh the way that animal was pawing me."

"What did he want?" I tried to ask evenly.

She winked at me. "You *know* what he wanted."

"Besides that?"

Peggy drifted into other areas such as the outrageous price of angora sweaters ($39.95 *on sale*) and peroxide (19¢ for a *tiny* bottle) for the hair, then asked if we could sneak a jug of whiskey up to her, past the bluenoses running the joint, prigs who didn't know how to have any fun.

We lied and said we'd try, made excuses, and got out of there.

At the front desk, I asked a woman in her fifties, "Has there been a very elderly gentleman named Ken Bolling been by to see Mrs. Smith?"

"Well, I wouldn't call him elderly. In his fifties isn't elderly, is it?"

"No, of course not," I said quickly. "Ken Bolling is in his *fifties*?"

"The older I get, the harder it is for me to judge a person's age, but he's no kid, though I don't think he's reached sixty." She ran a finger down her sign-in sheet. "Ken Bolling Junior. He's been here but doesn't stay along. He does not seem a happy camper when he leaves."

"How often?"

"Once a week. Twice a week. Twice a month. It varies."

I asked for a description.

"Tall and thin and a sour expression. Sharp dresser, you know, if you like the Vegas lounge lizard style like my ex was. The kind that'll feed you a line and have one hand inside your skirt and the other in your purse before you can say *pardon me, sir*. That's all I can think of. Mr. Bolling was in and out of here fast."

"Contact information?"

"None. We don't require it if a person's on the approved list. If Mrs. Smith hadn't said it was okay, we wouldn't've allowed him to visit."

Chapter 30

A Faraway Aunt

"IN THE 1950'S, IF THERE WAS AN UNWANTED pregnancy of an unmarried teen, the young woman went away to live with an 'aunt', an indulgent and loving woman who lived on the opposite coast," Fred Hudson told us back at the office. "Then, in seven or eight months or so, she came back home as if nothing had happened, although everyone knew it had. A charade bought into by all involved."

"Fred's right," Gramma Darla said. "It became a sick joke. At the first bout of morning sickness, the girl missed school because of the flu. When she missed her next period, the aunt or whomever was notified. Not everyone had such a helpful aunt, so off they went to a home for unwed mothers."

"Sounds Dickensian," I said, me a smarty-pants college grad.

"Indeed it was. Many were and still are operated by religious societies."

"The baby?" Abigail asked.

"Customarily adopted out."

I said, "Peggy had a fling with Bolling as well as King, two-timing the boss. Herbie may have known about Bolling also. When King got out of prison, he divorced her. She was already pregnant with Ken Junior."

Abigail said, "Peggy hasn't spoken of a child."

Fred said, "Perhaps she has blocked it out. As you have said, her mind drifts. Childlessness is a component, even if her only child visits her."

Abigail said, "An only child who perhaps winds up in an orphanage or a series of foster homes. He stews for years and blames people responsible for the unraveling of his parents and for his terrible childhood."

"Namely Herbert Allen Barnwell and my grandfather," I said. "Let's see if Detective Harrison is interested in any of this."

"He'd damn well better be," said Gramma Darla, gettingup.

Chapter 31

Kenneth Bolling (1926-1977)

DETECTIVE HARRISON was less than mildly interested in our theories and conclusions as he ran Kenneth Bolling on his computer, records his system had that weren't available to the general public after a person's death.

"I have a hit here. Has to be our boy. Kenneth Bolling missed a turn and ran off a Pierce Country road on Friday, May 13, 1977, an unlucky Friday the Thirteenth for him. He smacked a tree head-on. Bolling went all the way through the windshield. His blood-alcohol was more alcohol than blood. Get this. Bolling was driving a 1957 DeSoto. That tank must've cut a wide swath through the woods, those tail fins slicing right through the brush."

"The obit shows him as a classic-and-antique car dealer. No further details. No funeral services. Next of kin a mother and older sister. No names or addresses given. No bouncing baby boy listed."

"No family linkage other than that?" I said.

"Nope. Not according to our records, which began and ended with the obit, as there was no suspicion of criminal activity."

Abigail said, "I don't suppose you can station an officer at the seniors' home to pick up Ken Bolling Junior for questioning the next time he drops by."

Harrison laughed at her manpower naiveté and said, "You don't-suppose correctly unless the alleged Ken Bolling Junior is wanted for a crime, which he isn't at this time. Not as far as we know."

"Maybe Ken Senior was a collector of classic-car hood ornaments, forget the fenders and the rest," I said.

"That's not a crime, Bates. Everybody has a hobby, some a whole lot weirder than that."

"His next of kin?" Abigail said.

"You mean like a son?"

"Yes."

"Also not a crime unless they're escaped axe murderers, so as far as Kenneth Bolling Junior and miscellaneous next-of-kin go, you have the same shoe leather and Internet access as I do, lady."

Chapter 32

Ken Bolling Junior

THE INTERNET DIDN'T YIELD a thing on the mother and older sister in the funeral announcement, and not anything useful much on our Ken Bolling Junior. Among Facebook's two billion members were Ken Bollings, Kenning Bollings, Ken Bollingers, and less likely combinations. None could be our boy.

We compiled a piece here and there from business journals, and determined that he'd owned a junkyard ten miles out of town that sold parts for vintage cars. Exotic parts or not, a junkyard was a junkyard was a junkyard, and the property was presently abandoned. Whatever it was at the time, Junior had faded from view.

Until now.

When we could spare the time, Abigail, Fred Hudson and I took turns watching the comings and goings at the seniors' complex. Gramma Darla insisted in getting into the act too; after all, she'd seen the original Bolling at Peggy's preliminary hearing, her the recipient of his red roses.

There were relatively few visitors at the seniors' complex, even on Sundays. That was good for us, sad for the residents. In ten days time, we had seven possibles — tall, thin men who didn't stay long and had unhappy body language.

Throughout the agency's history, each investigator at the Linus Aalborg Detective Agency had a connection at DMV. We ran the plates we'd accumulated on the seven.

Zilch on Ken Bolling or a name remotely similar.

A possible visitor Gramma Darla had spotted registered in her memory as a possible Kenneth Bolling Junior.

It had been eons ago since she'd seen Senior at the hearings, she said, but there was a faint family resemblance, a disreputable slickness to him. His car was parked on the next block, so she got there fast enough to see that it was a mile-long 1991 Buick in "piss-poor condition", but didn't get there fast enough to catch the license plate.

Our DMV search for a Bolling who drove an ancient Buick geezermobile: zilch.

That afternoon, we sat around a table at our favorite bar, a dive named the Dugout Tavern on East Marginal Way South. Gramma Darla said that it had a fascinating history my grandfather knew well. The Dugout's bathtub gin and bookmaking were in its past. Cigarette smoke too; no smoking was permitted in public establishments in this state, to the outrage of the bulk of Dugout regulars.

The Dugout did retain a seediness Gramma Darla found endearing. The menu had expanded somewhat from the olden day's sole offering: popcorn. You took your chances on the food, though, and there were no microbrews on tap. If they ever hung up a fern, though, she said we were walking.

"Our guy Ken is antsy," Abigail said. "If he knows the seniors' home is being watched, he might never come back."

"Bingo!" I cried. "A Vital Mystery Clue."

"A vital what?" Abigail said.

"Do they play bingo here now?" Gramma Darla said.

"His name," I said.

164

"Ken Bingo?" Gramma Darla said. "What's in your beer, boy?"

"Kenneth Jones," I said. "Jones is Peggy's maiden name."

Fred said, "Peggy and the faraway aunt had to supply a last name when the child was born. Jones is logical."

We chugalugged our beer and hustled back to the empty office.

There are three formal motorways in Albania.

I got to work on our DMV contacts. There were no shortages of Kenneth Jones and 1991 Buicks, but there were only fourteen of the biggest '91 Buicks, the Park Avenue model, registered to a Kenneth Jones. Of those 14, just one lived in town. The others were spread throughout the state.

We found the local Buick parked in the lot of a shabby apartment house south of town, on Martin Luther King Way, an arterial fast filling with immigrants. Ethnic grocery stores were lettered in languages I'd never seen.

We parked at an edge of the lot.

"Now what?" I wondered out loud.

"We can't have a SWAT team sent in," Abigail said. "Detective Harrison is being mulish."

"Why not?" Gramma said.

"Probable cause," Hudson said.

"What a bunch of bat guano," Gramma said. "Kenneth Jones and his lack of probable cause is probably not done killing."

Likely not done, I thought. Gramma Darla might be next on his list.

"Shall we start a schedule again here?" Abigail said. "See where he goes?"

"If we do, for how long? Follow him to the grocery store and so forth?" Gramma said. "I'm developing blisters on my bony ass."

"I guess we wait for as long as it takes," I foolishly said.

"Oh, for Heaven's sake! If we wait for Harrison to get his legal ducks in a row, if Bolling answers his door at all, he'll read him his Miranda card far too late. The bastard will already be lawyered up."

"So?"

She sighed in exasperation. "This Miranda folderol. If you tell a hardened criminal he has the right to remain silent, the son of a bitch *will* remain silent. Common sense went right out the window when Miranda came along."

Chapter 33

Gramma Darla/Ms. Bates

GRAMMA DARLA WAS OUT OF THE CAR before we could rebut her logic or physically stop her (risking a bony elbow to the chops). She marched up to Kenneth Bolling/Jones's apartment and pounded on the door.

Kenneth opened it and peeked out. Gramma had him by an ear before he could react, pulling him downward, calling him everything but a nice guy.

She had him on his knees, saying, "You aren't a dead ringer for your daddy, young man, but up close and personal, you have the same shifty eyes and don't get me started on the weed-killer cologne."

Bolling was sobbing now. "Why did my mother give me up? Why?"

"Those were different times, young man. You did what you had to do. Is that why you kill people, to get in her good graces?"

"I visit her at the old folks home and she pretends she doesn't even know me! I once said I'd rent a larger apartment so she could move in with me. I can't repeat what she said to that. What she wanted is against the law."

"Incest?"

"In every small detail."

We rushed to Gramma Darla/Ms. Bates's assistance, although she didn't seem to need any. Abigail got on the horn with Detective Harrison. If Bolling was going to do a Perry Mason number, a complete confession by the defendant in the final act of the old TV series, we needed the law here and the perp Mirandized. Gramma gave us a profane editorial on *Miranda v. Arizona* and reluctantly agreed.

I sat on him and waited.

Perry Mason was exactly what transpired, beginning as Detective Harrison snapped the cuffs on. Bolling spilled all, how he blamed his victims for his miserable life. He gave permission to search his home without a warrant.

One more 1957 DeSoto Adventurer hood ornament was in plain sight, on a scruffy coffee table, utilized as nothing but a jungle gym for the ants crawling on it. Obviously, he didn't entertain often, nor spruce the place up for those nonexistent guests.

"Those who live by the hood ornament die by —"

"Brick," Abigail said, using that tone of hers.

I shut up.

"Bolling, you rascal," Gramma said. "It had my name on it, didn't it?"

"You ruined my father's life too, all of you!"

"This is rich," Detective Harrison said. "Let's go downtown and get this on paper so everybody can enjoy it."

Chapter 34

Family Reunion

D ARLA GAVE HER HUSBAND his daily goodbye-for-now kiss.

His eyes opened.

He squinted, blinked, and said raspingly, "I was napping. Did I oversleep?"

"Oh my God," she cried. "Yes, yes, my dear, you were napping."

"How long? Did I miss any appointments?"

"You overslept by eighty-one days, ten hours, thirty-five minutes, and four seconds."

"How? What? Why?"

She looked at his hair, which had gone from gray to pure white. "A long story."

He looked at one of his arms. "No green scales."

"What, dear?"

"Your magical kisses did the trick."

Abigail called in the puzzled medicos.

They filled the room, even more puzzled, especially after Gramps' self-diagnosis of a princess curing a frog princess.

Gramma Darla looked at the doctors and said, "Do you boys have a better idea?"

They didn't.

"I've got a killer headache," Gramps Brick said. "What the hell was I drinking last night?"

"Glucose," I said.

Darla phoned, summoning all other loved ones, even reclusive Brick Bates II, who had to be escorted by yours truly as he refused to drive, saying (truthfully?) that his

169

license had expired.

"How's the agency running, kiddo?"

"Fine. Couldn't be better."

The beginning and end of our small talk.

Many tears, much laughter. Many gentle hugs, as if he were porcelain.

Or enclosed in an eggshell.

~ ~ ~

Abigail and I had celebratory drinks at the Dugout on the way home.

Halfway there, on a residential street of modest pre-war homes, Abigail slammed on the brakes and ordered me out of the car.

She then dropped to one knee on the sidewalk and asked for my hand in marriage.

Inside a white picket fence, a wide-eyed lady in her seventies was watering her yard.

I accepted.

"Good for you, young man," she said.

When we got home, Abigail settled a dispute between two condo owners that had nearly escalated into a Wild West confrontation on the sport court, accusing each other of parking in front of the other's garage.

We went inside and made it as far as the living room floor and couch, and celebrated with a night of premarital sex. There was thunder and lightning outside, reminding us of the storm in Quito when we partook of similar debauchery. We lasted the night without gasping for breath, as we had at the Ecuadorian capital's 9350-foot altitude.

Next day, I did my part. I went into deep hock to buy her a wedding set. The engagement ring was a so-so 1.4-carat conflict-free yellow diamond.

We'll set a date after Gramps Brick is back on his feet and 100-percent.

~ ~ ~

Gramma Darla unplugged her son's cable TV box, laid it in the shower, and turned the water on.

Now that he's been weaned from his HDTV and gone through withdrawal, my father will be available to the Aalborg Detective Agency as a forensic consultant.

~ ~ ~

Detective Juan Diego Harrison submitted his retirement papers at the police department. He'll be coming to work for me at the agency, although I'm not sure any more who's the boss.

And don't care.

He'll be a rainmaker, bringing plenty of work with him from contacts he'd made over the years.

Chapter 35

The End

KENNETH JONES WAS BEING HELD without bail, awaiting trial. A series of absurd motions to dismiss by his attorney, a bombastic and ambulance-chasing Logan Spliff Junior, were denied. A newspaper reporter wrote that the judge was wearing out his gavel on Spliff.

I was a hero around the office. The gig didn't bill a penny, but we got a ton of ink that brought in clients by the droves.

I tended to administration until Mrs. Leo (Erlene) Spotts called me and said that her hubby's jealous streak wore off and he was straying again.

"Tomcatting", as she told me. "Chippy chasing."

When I went out the door on the job, there was not a wink or a smirk.

Nary a one.

❄   ❄   ❄

Thank you for reading.
Please review this book. Reviews help others find
Absolutely Amazing eBooks and inspire us to keep
providing these marvelous tales.

If you would like to be put on our email list to receive
updates on new releases, contests, and promotions,
please go to AbsolutelyAmazingEbooks.com and sign
up.

About the Author

Gary Alexander has written nearly a score of novels, including *Loot,* fourth in the mystery series featuring comic Buster Hightower. *Disappeared*, the first in the series, has been optioned to Universal Studios. And *Dragon Lady*, his Vietnam novel, was recently published.

He's written 150+ short stories and sold travel articles to 6 major dailies. One story appeared in *Best American Mystery Stories 2010*, another in *Ice Cold*, last year's Mystery Writers of America anthology.

Alexander is a nonsmoking, nondrinking vegetarian. He does, however, abuse caffeine and chocolate.

His website is www.garyralexander.net.

The New Atlantian Library

NewAtlantianLibrary.com
or AbsolutelyAmazingEbooks.com
or AA-eBooks.com